Drown
them in the Sea

NICHOLAS ANGEL grew up on a property in western Queensland. He completed his law degree in Brisbane and did a masters in international law at a French university. He is currently working for an international law firm in Paris. His passions include rugby, cricket and fishing, playing the guitar and travelling. *Drown them in the Sea* is his first book.

NICHOLAS ANGEL

Drown
them in the Sea

ALLEN&UNWIN

First published in 2004

This project has been assisted by the Commonwealth
Government through the Australia Council, its arts funding
and advisory board.

Allen & Unwin
83 Alexander Street
Crows Nest NSW 2065
Australia
Phone: (61 2) 8425 0100
Fax: (61 2) 9906 2218
Email: info@allenandunwin.com
Web: www.allenandunwin.com

National Library of Australia
Cataloguing-in-Publication entry:

Angel, Nicholas, 1978–.
    Drown them in the sea.

    ISBN 1 74114 349 7.

    1. Farm life – Australia – Fiction. I. Title.

A823.3

Set in 11/15 pt Adobe Garamond by Asset Typesetting Pty Ltd
Printed in Australia by McPherson's Printing Group

10 9 8 7 6 5 4 3 2 1

To my Grandparents

It crushed them . . . until they perceived themselves finite and small, specks and motes moving with weak cunning and little wisdom amidst the play and interplay of the great blind elements and forces.
Jack London

Standing tall on the sand ridge the dog looked out over the flats below and saw a faraway header working up and down the length of a wheat paddock like a tiresome red ant. It sprayed yellow grain dust up onto a canvas of high November sky and blotted over the distant tree line showing blue and hazy. He was a big red mongrel with scars along his muzzle. There was kelpie in his pointed ears, blue heeler in the way he worked close on cattle, collie in the white stripes, maybe some labrador or German shepherd in his box head, and a good streak of dingo. The dingo in him made him run away. He'd run away for days at a time, up the river or out through the sand-ridge country, get right into the native calm, under the awnings of the old trees and let the dingo off the chain for a while. The dingo in him spoke with a voice the other breeds listened to. He was out in the river block now with the tallest trees he knew, all full of squawks and song like the dingo in him. It sang in his soul under those trees and he ran with it.

Down by the river he followed a pad of kangaroo prints set from the last solid rain. The pad ran through tall grasses burnt brown down to the very base of each clump. He went between towering old gum trees and down an eroded gully of high walls beside the river, past bright evergreen clumps of saw grass and burnt stumps. The charcoal was familiar. He recognised it as part of the bush smell. He had run all morning, full of song, in amongst the big old tangled river trees. Presently he came upon a thickly treed flat where kangaroos and wallabies assembled in the late afternoon. There was nothing there now.

And then he came upon another bare flat. This one backed away from the river and away from the trees and that was where the singing in him stopped and the other dogs in him came out and sent the dingo off. He headed towards the bare flat and some time later he ambled under a fence standing behind two silver grain silos. The silos were set on the edge of a large clearing in which a small house was central. A modest shed, a coolroom, stables, several kennels and a rickety windmill gave the isolated little conglomerate a sense of civilisation.

He saw his master in the outer shed, and wagging his tail, he trotted under the shade of the shed and lay down to pant out of the heat.

'G'day mate,' Millvan said. 'Where have you been?'

The dog thumped up dust with his tail and smiled.

Millvan watched his dog settle then went back to his work.

He was changing one of the ute tyres which had finally blown a valve and no amount of foam or plugs could fix it.

There was blood over his hand and grease on his shirt. He'd knocked off the skin when the spanner whipped off a burred nut. He saw some flies perched still on the blood but kept working regardless.

He didn't complain about flies or blood and it showed in the way he looked. His small nose was flat and his ears cauliflowered. He had thick grey hair and at times his eyes matched either his khaki shirts or blue work shorts. They were bright eyes but the sun had pushed them into permanent slits and when he looked out at the glare from the shed the rest of his face wrinkled in contortion. He was tall, built thick, and wore heavy boots. His well-worn Akubra had a tear in the peak of its crown.

Millvan owned the river property known as Arbour and wanted nothing more than for his son to take it over just as he'd taken it from his father thirty years ago. He didn't want to leave, because it was his place to run, and as far as Millvan was concerned, the only place fit for him. He hadn't been around but he did know the way of things. The way of things meant his son *would* take over. It was as sure as the sun goes down and simple as a blue sky. The way of things said that his son's shoulders would widen and that in time Millvan would leave. The thought of leaving made him sad but it was part of a process he believed in. He loved his Arbour but he'd leave it too.

Meanwhile, he'd wake up earlier and farm and fix and work and sell and hopefully he'd save enough money to buy a small house by the sea. That was what he wanted when his back finally gave in or his hands lost their will. He'd pile all their things into a truck and leave his son behind in its dust to shut the barking dogs up.

He finished with the tyre and stood up. It was nearly summer, and the end of harvest; the last load of wheat had been augured up into the silos. This was the first time in six years the silos had held grain; for six years they'd just creaked and boomed when it got really hot. Now they stood quiet.

He'd done most of the harvest by himself and hadn't seen a crack in time since he'd started filling those damn things. *Still, they look better full,* he assured himself, smiling. *I bet no one's ever seen such good-looking full silos. That was a good harvest that one, very good but very long.*

He stretched his back and wrinkled his face to look over at the silos. 'Who's creaking and booming now?'

He was always glad when things got done. The harvest was done and now the ute was ready for the long drive into town in the morning.

He left the shed for the house. It was an old Queens-lander with an encircling verandah. On the verandah were decent chairs to sit in. Shady peppercorns sheltered the western aspect from the evening sun, and out the front was one bald old box tree with rattle leaves only in its highest branches. The dingo followed him. Three dogs trotted out to greet them as they walked to the house. They were half-breed work dogs, blue heelers, kelpies and the like, and when they weren't working they barked whenever cars came in.

Halfway there he stopped in the clearing and spent several long minutes looking to the north where some thin cirri hung like wires in an old fence. He was still thinking about the weather he'd seen in the sky when he stomped up the steps to the house and along the verandah. He heard his wife Michelle sing out something to him and after he'd washed up he found there was a pot of coffee waiting on the kitchen table.

'So is the wheat finished then?' she asked with hands on hips.

Millvan wiped at water trickling from his wet hair and rubbed his eyes. He didn't answer.

'You need a good rest,' she said. 'Why don't you lie down for a while?'

'Nah,' he said, sitting down and helping himself to the coffee. He looked up at her rounded face. She had strong arms and hair the colour of stubble.

'You've hardly slept in three weeks,' she implored.

'Sean's taken off the last corner,' he said, looking around the wooden kitchen, 'so you'll have to write him out his pay cheque when he comes in later on.' Sean was the header driver from New Zealand.

'This is day twenty-three, isn't it?'

'Yes, love,' he said. 'His contract and rates are by the wireless.'

'I'll sort it out,' she said, 'but why don't you go have a lie-down now?'

'I've got to help him pack away the header comb and run some cattle out of the river block. I haven't looked at the cattle for ages. What's Murray up to?'

Murray was their eldest son. Terry was the youngster still in school. Murray was home from ag college and had taken the morning off to do assignments.

'Oh he's around somewhere. Which reminds me— Donny said he might come down later on.'

'Is he bringing Flynn?'

'I'd say so.'

Donny was one of Millvan's best friends but a lot of people couldn't hack him. He'd spent a lot of time in the army before coming home to work on Satang as a farmer. He'd jagged lucky storms all through the drought and sometimes Millvan wondered if he'd swapped something for a lot of luck in Vietnam. Flynn hadn't got as many storms as Donny but had made it through the drought better than both Millvan and Donny. He was a breeder of fine cattle and didn't grow grain crops. The few storms he'd jagged were enough to keep his breeders fed, and the healthy cattle market spread a protective wing over his livelihood. He was well liked by all but was a much better lifter than thinker. The three of them were old mates.

Millvan smiled. 'Hopefully we'll all get a hit out of the storm front coming down.'

'What front?'

'There's one coming down from the Central Highlands.'

'I haven't heard anything mentioned on the radio,' she said, pouring herself some coffee.

'What do they know about it?' he said. 'The easterly has been blowing since Wednesday morning and Dad always said that meant an inch in November.' There was a moment's silence. 'Gee it'd be nice so soon after harvest.'

'Yes,' she answered earnestly. In such intermittent country propped up by ephemeral scrub, rain was the colour, a smile, a holiday from the dry and heat. It flushed the river and made the frogs sing by the thousands in the evenings. She liked it when the big frog chorus put her off to sleep.

'*A week from the east is an inch at least,*' sang Millvan.

'And wet roads'd be a good excuse to avoid the bank tomorrow,' she said.

Millvan smiled with the corners of his eyes as he finished his coffee. 'Murray,' he yelled. Murray came into the kitchen, stooping through the doorway.

'Put your boots on,' said Millvan.

Murray did as he was told. Millvan got up and followed him out of the kitchen.

By mid afternoon they'd helped Sean finish packing away the header's comb. After that Millvan took Murray out to one of the back paddocks to check a fence. They had to strain a wire and change half-a-dozen batons. Cattle must have hit the fence, or maybe kangaroos.

'Dad?' asked Murray.

'What?'

'How come goats can get through a fence but not sheep?'

'They're wild,' said Millvan. 'You see goats and you shoot them.'

'Why?'

'Because they're dirty, and covered in lice and ticks.'

'Why don't sheep get lice?' he asked.

'Because we shoot the goats.'

Murray still had a lot to learn. Millvan had always taken him along with him whenever he could. Whether it was finding a busted pipe with a water wand or going over old things like operating the cultivator, the boy had to learn.

They drove their bikes down to the next paddock. It had occurred to Millvan that he ought to move cattle from one paddock to another smaller river block. With Murray's help he could easily shift them through before dark. They found the cattle scattered between the river and a clump of kurrajong. They picked up the few in the clump and that became the head and tail of the mob. The others were easy to pick up and they went together walk-trotting towards the gate under a big cloud of dust. It was looking to be simple until a bullock decided it wouldn't be pushed around and broke away. It'd been the one holding a high head in the mob. Millvan wasn't worried. Cattle always broke away. The other cattle ignored it and continued towards the gate. Millvan putted over to Murray and told him to keep them ambling whilst he brought the rogue back.

Murray nodded.

Millvan made a fast circle to get behind the runaway beast. He drove in fifth across the cultivation and it jarred his lungs. The bullock ignored him.

'Go back, you bastard!' he yelled from in front of it.

It kept trotting towards him.

Millvan rushed the bullock fast in low gear so that the bike screamed. Normally the noise turned them but the bullock held its course and seemed to push faster as the bike whizzed past.

'YOU MONGREL!'

Millvan tried rushing it again but it wouldn't turn, and when he got close to it he had to pull away suddenly because the bullock had half a mind to charge. Both times it went on snorting over the sound of the bike. It was whipping its tail around and its eyes were showing white. Millvan knew he probably couldn't turn it. The bullock had a temperament and soon it was running flat out. Before long they were quite a way from the others.

'Turn, you bastard!' he yelled. But the more he pushed it, the angrier he got. The angrier he got, the more he yelled and the faster it ran. They were at a gallop when Millvan realised that he'd sent the bullock's brains to its feet. That was the way of things with cattle: their brains fell to their feet in flat open country. He'd stop it in timber but not out on the cultivation.

Millvan slowed the bike and let the bullock disappear behind the dust of its hooves.

It'll run half a mile before it stops, he thought to himself. He looked at the sky. The light had got to fading. He decided to cut out a handful of timid steers. There'd be just enough time to let them wander back to meet up with the bullock and nanny it into their herd. Millvan looked at the sky again. There'd be time but the bullock had to calm and get its breath.

In the meantime he could push the main mob of cattle ahead into the smaller river block.

He drove back to the mob. He went slower over the cultivation but it still jarred his lungs. He found Murray not far from the gate. He'd handled the mob slowly. Together they cut out a dozen or so cattle from the tail to run back and nanny the runaway. They were heavy bullocks, fat and puffing. They trotted away, bellies swinging, in the direction of the rogue.

He drove the cattle faster. The mob stepped up from an amble to a trot and brought up even more dust from the ground. They made the gate and Murray stopped his bike. He got off it and slowly walked around the edge of the mob as Millvan kept the cattle milling in front of the gate. He opened the gate and walked through it to show the cattle. One ran through nervously, then others hurried to catch it, and before long the whole mob had poured through and was cavorting on the other side. Millvan turned off his bike so the lowing and tight thunder of the hooves was the only sound. The long twilight had all but faded and the dust came up red from under them. Millvan fixed the gate open with a forked stick after the stragglers had walked into the river paddock as far as Murray could throw a stone.

They walked back to their bikes, listening as the lowing mob got further away.

'Why'd you cut off those end ones, Dad?'

'So we could bring the mongrel back. It's easier to work ten cattle than one by itself.'

'Couldn't you get it?'

Millvan started his bike again and didn't answer. He motioned for Murray to follow. They drove down the cattle pad along the edge of the cultivation. Before long they saw the bullock feeding with the other handful of cattle. The bullock stood three hands taller than they did. It had its head up again and was watching the bikes approach with wide eyes. Then its head ducked under the swinging bellies and looked out through their legs. The bullock snorted but the heavies squeezed around it and moved it with them. The two bikes putted in slowly behind the little mob. They drew a wide flank and Millvan motioned to Murray with his palm to go slowly. As the bikes came closer the fat bullocks pushed the rogue with them. The bikes closed in on them steadily until the little mob came to the edge of the cultivation. Then the bullock pushed and bucked and broke away again.

'You bastard!' Millvan yelled.

The rest of the little mob was left to feed on the pluck clover as the bikes followed fast after the bullock.

Murray heard Millvan swearing over both of the engines. He swore himself. 'Mongrel of a thing.' He didn't know how they were going to turn it.

The light filtering through the bullock's dust was a thin blue now. The bullock ran as hard as it had before and ignored both Millvan's curses and his attempts to turn it.

Murray drove behind them and waited for his father's signal. He watched Millvan zag the bike well in front of the bullock then jackknife the bike around and drive headlong at it. Millvan was standing up on the bike and waving his Akubra. Murray watched as his father got within a cricket pitch of the cantering bullock.

Millvan sat down on his bike and wrenched the left handlebar down as the bullock charged. It came wide-eyed and head up and, as he pulled to the left, it passed to the right of his father. Murray accelerated towards it to prevent it breaking free again. He heard Millvan yell 'HOHH' as the bullock cantered past.

Murray held his acceleration and promptly found himself alongside the galloping bullock's flank. He saw white foam clinging to its muzzle, and dull horns. He was still accelerating when he tried to turn it.

Millvan turned his bike to follow them and watched his son come in fast to the shoulder and on a bad angle. The bullock was cantering and swung its head to see the new noise, its big brown pupils whitened. It snorted and then, still cantering, charged and collected him. Millvan saw the maroon blur of the beast going over him, the red bike, and then Murray falling and the bullock bolting off. The bump had scared it. He saw his son lying still behind wheeling dust.

Murray's head was opened up and the bike whined as it lay on its side. It was still in gear. Bits of dirt flicked up from the back wheel. By the time Millvan had killed the bike, the rogue had made off through the far trees. Millvan could still smell the strong bullock. Murray had pushed himself up onto one knee. He was moaning, and both hands were already bloody from touching at his head. One of his eyes was shut up with red dirt. He'd split his pants falling off the bike and Millvan could see one knee was grazed. Blood and dirt were indiscriminately mixed. Millvan ripped his own shirt sleeve off to make a wad and pushed it gently onto the bad cut.

'Hold it there.'

Under the pressure blood spread slowly through the cloth.

'C'mon we're going home.'

'How can I drive?' Murray asked, with his hands on his head. His eyes had lost their ability to focus.

'Get on the back of mine. You'll be all right.'

Murray's tongue lolled in his mouth and his eyes blinked slowly and dumbly.

He'll be all right, Millvan told himself, even though Murray slipped on the seat.

'It's all right,' Millvan said to him. 'We're going home. You'll be all right. Are you on?'

Murray gripped one arm around his father's waist.

They left the other bike where it lay. The front wheel had been folded under the frame and the tank was dinged. They passed the heavies back near the gate. They scattered them as they drove past and then shut the gate.

He'll be all right once Michelle tends to him, Millvan repeated to himself.

It wasn't as bad as when he got burnt scalding the porkers.

He asked Murray if he needed to stop for a bit.

'No, but I can't move my shoulder.'

'Can you hold on?'

'Yeah I reckon.'

He couldn't see if he was all right so he talked to him instead.

'You'll be all right, mate. What do you think? Hey?'

Murray had his eyes closed and grunted.

'It's just not your day and you copped a hiding,' he said loudly. 'We all cop a hiding sometime, little mate, and that's just the way of things. You'll be all right though, my little mate. You're tough and that makes me proud as punch. Hang on, mate, we're nearly there. You still all right, mate?'

By the time they got in, the dark had come out of the trees.

They parked the bike in the machinery shed then Millvan helped Murray to the house. He saw the blood had stopped flowing but it was the concussion that worried him.

As they walked into the house yard they saw Donny Graw's ute.

Millvan lift-walked Murray up the stairs and his boots resounded heavily.

'Here he is!' yelled a guttural voice. Millvan knew it was Flynn. When they walked into the kitchen they saw Donny, Sean and Flynn sitting at the kitchen table.

'How does it feel to finish?' asked Donny jovially. Then he saw Murray and his eyes sharpened.

'Holy shit, boy!'

'I got hit,' he said, his eyes still dumb. 'I came in too quickly.'

'Where's Michelle?' asked Millvan.

No one answered so he yelled for her. The men all stared at Murray. He kept his arm around Millvan's shoulder.

'Did your life flash before your eyes?' said Flynn, trying to lighten the situation.

'Nah, I'm not dead,' he told them. 'I'll be all right.'

They smiled but Donny cursed softly when he saw the cut. At that very moment Michelle arrived in a whirlwind of panic and whisked Murray off to the bathroom.

'*Good Jesus . . . where* was your father?' Millvan made to go with her but she shooed him away. He sighed and went back to the kitchen.

'Did he come a gutser?' asked Sean.

Millvan shook his head. 'Nah, a bullock cleaned him up and hell knows how he came out better than the bike. I reckon it was one of them obstinate yaks you sold me, Donny.'

Flynn laughed. 'That'd be right! Half of 'em are mickey bulls.' He was a hulking man who liked fights. There was grease on his freckly arms and permanent stains on his hands. He was probably Millvan's best mate; they'd known each other since they were little buggers.

'Sit down and have a drink with us,' said Donny, ignoring them, 'now that we've all finished harvest.'

Millvan got a beer but continued to pace around the kitchen.

'He'll be right as rain when she finishes with him,' soothed Donny. 'Probably just concussion is all.'

'But he can't move his shoulder.'

'Well lucky his mother was a nurse,' replied Donny.

Millvan nodded briefly then he shook his head again. 'Jeez he was lucky.'

'He'll be right,' said Donny, waving it aside, 'he'll be right.' He quaffed down his beer and opened another one, throwing the cap out the window. 'Sit down.'

Millvan stared back at them. Flynn was watching him anxiously.

Just then there was a knocking on the door and Dave and Will Larkham came into the kitchen. They looked very drunk and were loud enough in their greetings to bring

Terry out from in front of the television. The young brothers occasionally worked for Flynn.

'I told them I'd be up here having a drink,' Flynn explained to Millvan.

'Come in, fellas,' said Millvan, waving them in. He saw Terry and told him to go feed the dogs. Terry trudged off reluctantly.

'We've all finished harvest,' said Will.

A few moments later Michelle came back into the kitchen and told them Murray was in bed. The Larkham boys hadn't had time to put down their hats. They held them with both hands and the crowns came out over their stomachs.

'G'day,' said Dave. Will nodded curtly.

'Hello,' was all she said, which was very unusual. She looked shook up and annoyed. She glanced around at them all sitting there, saw the bottles and the drunken boys, then told them to take it all outside.

'Eh?'

'Murray's got a pretty bad concussion,' she said, 'which means he's got a hell of a headache to go with it. I'm going to have to keep a close eye on him, and it'd be better if you took the noise outside. You lot would be more comfortable on the verandah where it's cooler anyway,' she said.

'Outside?' Flynn whined. 'You know we've *all* gotta have a drink at the end of harvest.' He looked around for support but they were smiley and uncomfortable, not sure if he was kidding.

'Get a glass and I'll fix you a brandy,' he went on. 'Michelle, you know he'll sleep well after a good knock to the head. I should know.'

'He needs a good sleep,' she said firmly.

'But what about the bugs? . . . We wouldn't wake him.'

She shook her head at him.

'C'mon fellas, we can build a fire and continue it out there,' said Millvan. 'We'll go and make a fire by the river like we did at Jacko's, you don't get bugs around a fire.'

'It'll be like Jacko's clearing sale,' said Donny. 'C'mon chaps.'

The boys were happy to put their hats back on and said they'd go look for wood.

Sean and Flynn made to go with them.

'I'm just going to check on Murray,' said Millvan. 'I'll be out in a minute. I'll find the fire easily if you get it started.' He gave Flynn an old newspaper and a tin of kerosene.

Flynn put his boots on and took the paper and the tin.

'Are you coming?' he asked Donny.

'I'm too old for that sort of thing.'

'Are you gunna go home?' asked Flynn.

'No, but we don't need that many blokes roaming in the dark looking for wood. I'll come out later with Millvan.'

Flynn tutted and shook his head.

Donny sat back down and smiled at him lazily. 'Go and get it started!'

Flynn smiled back and left down the stairs. He was

happy Donny wasn't going home. Flynn had been looking forward to this end of harvest drink.

Donny looked over at Millvan. He looked very tired and was still pacing around.

'You know, I read somewhere today they're trying to—'

Millvan cut him off. 'I'll be back in a sec, mate.' He headed off to the bedroom at the end of the breezeway to check on Murray.

Donny sipped his beer. Shame about that yak. The boy was normally good with cattle too. Millvan needed a beer. He opened one for him. Get his mind off things.

The others were finding the night too dark to find wood easily. They walked in under the trees by the river to find branches and stumps then dragged them out into the clearing next to Millvan's old disc plough. The moon reflected dim silver from the roofs of the sheds but it couldn't penetrate down under the trees, the night there was darker than their pupils. In the branches of the trees were webs strung by golden-orb weavers, and down by the river the night was full of crickets and frog sounds. Dave and Will went together and found very little. Flynn and Sean could not see one another but each knew where the other was from the cracking of busted sticks under their boots. Loud cracks echoed when they split branches. Once Flynn pulled a dead branch off a low box tree and an echo came back off from one of the sheds. After a short time they'd dragged in a lot of wood and three big logs to sit on. Flynn heaped the wood into a pile. Then he found his tin and tipped fuel over the pile, struck a match and whooshed the fire going. Dave and Will carried the eskies over from beside the disc plough and used them as seats. Flynn and Sean sat on the logs.

Donny started talking as soon as Millvan got back.

'Harvest is done with,' said Donny, 'the clouds are banking up for summer rains and Murray'll be all right—just relax will you. What do you think we're here for?'

'To have a drink I suppose.'

'Yeah,' he said, 'and . . .'

'Harvest is over . . . the grain is in the silos, what else?'

'Rawlings?'

'What about him?' snapped Millvan.

'Don't sit there and pretend we don't know. Flynn's been . . . I should've let him bring this up.' Donny stopped and sipped slowly; for a few seconds there was heavy silence save for the crickets. Millvan stared ahead with glassy eyes.

'Michelle told us you were going in to see him tomorrow.'

Millvan shook his head softly.

'It's not her fault,' said Donny.

Millvan began squeezing the bridge of his nose between thumb and forefinger. 'We'll make it through,' he said gruffly.

'You're not the only one, mate,' said Donny, 'it's happening all over the place. The good season made people's places worth a bit and banks are picking up what they haven't had for a good long time.'

'I don't know yet.'

'And Rawlings . . .?' Donny began.

Jonathon Rawlings was the branch manager for the bank that handled all the big farm loans. He was a familiar topic for everyone in the community. Half hated him, the other half tried to please him. He had become a wealthy man from his connections, and the people who hated him thought he took interest on his friendships as well as his loans.

'Rawlings will tell me how it is tomorrow,' said Millvan.

'Which is why we're here,' said Donny. 'It's Flynn's idea.'

Millvan smiled warmly but only for an instant.

'He's a good one,' said Millvan.

'He'd just about give you a hand before he'd help himself. Anyway, we'll help speed things up around here if Rawlings needs you to get a move on.'

Millvan smiled quickly again. 'But tell me, though, what did Michelle say to you two?'

'She said you weren't sleeping and that she thought it was because you might need a hand.'

'So she invited you over tonight?'

'Nah, that was Flynn's idea; she's kicked us out, remember?'

Millvan nodded. 'Donny,' he started, 'this Rawlings business is probably nothing much. All I know is that he's been trying to get me to go in there and see him and I've been putting it off, don't ask me why. It's probably nothing but . . .'

'You'll see soon enough,' said Donny.

Millvan drained the last of his bottle and nodded.

'If you need a hand . . .'

'Thanks Donny,' said Millvan. He changed the subject. 'So what are you going to do with all your fattened bullocks?'

'Dunno, wait till I can sell the bastards.'

'We sold most of ours,' said Millvan. 'Only two good mobs left.'

'Didn't save them for a rainy day?'

'Already too many things to do when it rains, rainy days are the busiest days of all.'

Donny laughed. 'Sounds about right actually.' He slapped dust from his trousers. 'I'm looking forward to some rain out of that front coming down though. Hey, did you hear there was a big climb in the market for pine?'

'Yeah, I heard that on the radio,' said Millvan. 'Pity the cattle market couldn't learn from it.'

Donny thought about bringing Rawlings up again but hesitated. Millvan could see it in his face. A lot of people couldn't put up with Donny and his Vietnam fits but at that moment Millvan was glad he'd taken the good with the bad. He knew he could rely on Donny if he ever needed him. He patted him on the back and they both sat quietly for a time and just sipped beer.

By the fire the others were drinking a little quicker than the two men inside. Flynn and Sean didn't know each other so they both drank quicker than was their custom, and since Flynn was Will and Dave's boss, they drank to keep up with him as a matter of dignity. Will moved off the esky so Flynn could take a beer and slipped as he sat backwards onto one of the logs.

The brothers wanted to know what had happened to Murray. Dave looked very concerned but Flynn shrugged it.

'The boy's been coddled.'

Flynn opposed weakness. That was why he forced the last few bottles of beer down come the end of a night. It made him fight playing pool and drive fast the whole way home from the pub.

'He needs a bit of rough and tumble knocked into him. All kids need it.'

Sean looked disgusted. 'Not that badly,' he said.

'My boys copped their share and you wouldn't argue with them, mate!'

'Rubbish,' said Dave. 'They left for the Territory because they couldn't handle it back here working with us.'

'If they were still here you wouldn't have a job, bucko,' Danny replied laughing.

'Up in the Territory, are they?' asked Sean.

'Yeah,' said Flynn. 'They both went up after their mum died.' He shook his big head sadly.

'Old Millvan works hard,' said Sean suddenly. 'He works as hard as any boss I've ever had.'

'That's our Millvan,' said Flynn. He smiled a big gapped-tooth smile.

'But what in the hell of a name is that?' asked Sean. 'Has he got a bit of something foreign in him?'

'What?' chuckled Flynn. 'He's pure as a merino lamb.'

'Is it a nickname or his real name?' asked Sean.

Dave and Will were interested because they didn't know either, but Flynn looked up at the stars and didn't reply. He was old enough to know the importance of a good pause, and so he took a good long look at the Milky Way, from Sagittarius to the Coalsack to Alfa Centauri. Besides, he could feel the rum already had a hold of him and used the time to remind himself of the story.

'How did he get to be Millvan?' yelled Will impatiently.

Flynn slowly looked down from the heavens. 'It was back in the sixties.'

'Don't you start talking sixties horseshit like Donny does,' said Dave.

'And don't you wet your nightie, girlie,' said Flynn. 'In those days we went to a lot of rodeos. This one time they trapped a wild bull into one of the yards. It was motley brindle, would have weighed in well over half a ton yet still had that rangy look about it because it came out of the hills. You know how the rangy ones are always the worst. This thing had horns too.'

'Big?' asked Will.

'Big and sharp.'

'Was Millvan the bull's name?' interrupted Dave.

'Listen boys, if you're going to make me tell you a little story you can fix me a little drink—my throat's getting dry.'

Dave leant back out of the way quickly, so Flynn turned to Will.

Will swayed as he took the cup from Flynn's huge hand. Everybody watched him slosh rum into the cup and hand it back.

'Anyway, this bull was snorting and carrying on in the yards and looked like a real ratbag of a thing. John Ducko laughed his arse off when Millvan drew it. You heard of John Ducko?'

Sean shook his head.

'He did fairly well on the bulls but not even he was up for a stint on that bull. Bloke had seen more horn than a French milkmaid and it wasn't like him to shy away.

'So Millvan went and inspected it and came back as white as an aspirin. He said to Ducko, "You can strike me pink and call me Dolly if I stay on this thing. I swear there's no way I'll ride it." He carried on about it to us too, but since none of us wanted to ride it either, we put up with him at first. Anyhow, our man took it on the chin but he bitched on and on about it. Really, we were just hoping the rodeo would start so the fucking bull could shut him up.'

Dave gave a sarcastic little laugh.

'You wouldn't have gone near it either, sonny,' warned Flynn.

Will sniggered.

'Anyway, finally it was his turn to ride and Millvan was so damn scared in the chute he started saying his prayers. While he was sitting up on that mean bull waiting for the gate to open he bowed his head down low and whispered prayers out over the bullock's ears—Hail Marys and Our Fathers. Those prayers hung in the air thick like farts, then—Bamm! He came out of the chute. Somehow he was still on him. He hung on and would you believe it, the brindle bastard never bucked a shoe. It gave a few lazy kicks and then trotted around the ring like an old milker. IT WAS A MIRACLE!'

'Give me back that drink!' yelled Will.

Flynn laughed with his big horsy-teeth head.

'The chute kid had passed out drunk and no one had tied the bells on it,' Flynn guffawed hard. 'A bull won't buck much without bells! Our Millvan wouldn't come down then. He started waving his hat around and played up to everyone so much they eventually pulled him off and threw him in the horse trough. He didn't get a score but that night he told everyone how he tamed the unrideable bull with a few whispers in the chute. Didn't he rub it in too, he said he was the Bull Whisperer!'

Sean and Dave smirked.

'That night in the bar Ducko was explaining to someone how he stayed on and Millvan butted in with something like, "you show ponies always win".'

'I bet I know what Ducko said,' interrupted Sean.

'Yeah, him and the rest of the bar. The only fucking injustice was that Millvan didn't cop a horn up the arse.

Then Ducko remembered what Millvan had said before he got on and told us all. We all started laughing at him and calling Millvan's bull a show pony and . . . because the bull's name was Millvan, somehow it stuck with him. It stuck better than Dolly, though we called him that for a while too. He probably won't remember, but call him Dolly and see what happens.'

'You said before it wasn't the bull's name!' said Dave?

'Well I lied then you little bugger!'

Flynn gulped down his rum.

Suddenly a loud and strangely accented voice yelled at them from the night. 'Halloo thar laddies, give up yer gold.'

'No, it's women then yer gold,' yelled Flynn into the darkness.

'Give up yer beer then,' came the voice again. It was closer now.

Flynn told it to piss off and they laughed.

Out of the dark emerged Donny and Millvan dragging another esky with them.

'Who here's got all the gold?' asked Donny.

'You're the one with the vineyard,' pointed Flynn.

'The only vines I have grow pumpkins, mate' replied Donny.

'You're posh enough to have a vineyard.'

'From the man who's drunk all my beer tonight,' said Donny with mock disgust. 'Now I have to drink that awful rum.'

27

'You love it!' They laughed with each other.

In the esky Millvan and Donny had brought were some sandwiches Michelle had made. They passed them around and for a moment there was no talk whilst they ate. Everybody looked into the breathing red obscurity and sipped on their beers. The fire lit up their faces. Millvan's was red, whilst Donny's appeared agitated, his temple furrowed and eyes full of an idea apparently hidden in the heart of the fire itself. Dave's eyes began to droop and Will's opened and shut gently in the battle to keep awake.

Flynn looked over at Millvan. He wanted to ask him how bad it was with Rawlings, but he decided Millvan would bring it up himself if he wanted to. He put it off till later.

After a time Sean spoke. 'I heard a story the other day,' he said cautiously. The others didn't blink away from the fire.

He finished chewing and then sipped at his drink. His eyes flicked around and he saw them all still staring into the fire.

'The other day when I was harvesting in the Gidgee they told me this story about a bloke who drove a bus . . .' No one looked up.

'. . . When he'd finished his run or it was a weekend, he tended bees. And whenever anyone got a swarm in their garden he would come and take them.'

Dave watched him with one eye open.

'A couple of months ago this bloke found a big angry hive down by the local cricket club and killed himself trying to rob them.'

'What, what, what?' asked Donny.

'They were living in a big hollow box tree that had all but fallen over.'

'Box tree? What were?'

He started again and this time they listened as they stared into the fire.

'They were living inside this huge hollow old tree and he had to smoke them out to get the honey. He built a little fire inside the base and piled green leaves on it to make the smoke. He did that then climbed up inside the shaky old limb to get at the honey. And then it collapsed on him.'

The others were listening carefully now.

'Poor bastard may well of been killed right there and then but in any case he was a goner because the tree was now a pile of dead wood on top of him.' Sean stopped and gasped a little, struggled to get it out. 'And because the fire came back.'

'Poor bastard,' said Donny quietly.

'It might have been an ember that caught on at night time, or maybe it started straightaway. Nobody knows because when they got there all they found were coals, rusty boot nails and a dinged-up screen mask. Seeing there was an empty can and a bee smoker near by, his poor wife had to put two and two together. She was the one who confirmed it. What a horrible thing to see.'

'Poor bastard would have had plenty of time for his life to flash before his eyes,' murmured Donny.

They were quiet for a long time, with only the crackling wood and the chugging of their bottles, before Flynn spoke.

'You think it actually does?'

'Everyone seems to say so,' said Donny.

'Who, all the dead people?' asked Sean.

'I think some memories do come back,' said Donny, 'but there's probably only time for the best few.'

'What if you get shot in the back of the head?' asked Flynn.

'Well you probably have a premonition.'

'Bullshit. When you're dead you're dead.'

Suddenly Dave was wide awake. 'I hope the poor bugger suffocated.'

'It'd be a better way to go than burning,' agreed Millvan.

'*If* he was still alive after the branch fell down,' added Donny. He looked pale. The story had triggered something in him.

'If you're stuck in a burn it's the smoke that kills you,' continued Dave, 'and I've even heard of people who suffocated without the smoke.'

'Yeah and so the air inside a circle of fire gets so thin you start dreaming. You see—'

'Smoke,' said Millvan sarcastically.

'Nah, women with big tam-tams,' said Dave. 'You dream 'cause there's no air.'

'The fire's one mercy,' added Donny softly. He looked white.

'The air gets sucked out of the circle and the bloke in the middle can't breathe.'

At this point they noticed Donny was humming and rocking gently on his log. Millvan and Flynn knew he could cry sometimes on the booze and Flynn motioned to the others to stay quiet and not to laugh. When Donny had first came back from Vietnam he'd had lots of fits, and farm machinery like tractors and bulldozers had triggered agitated moments of rocking and crying, his eyes clenched shut like his fists. But the worst trigger of all was the booze. The war had stayed with him and sometimes when he was drunk it would make him cry and rock in his chair. There was nothing they could do to stop him for it was very deep inside him. He was too deep in his war to hear you tell him to stop when he got like that. So they kept on drinking around him. Normally after five minutes or so he would stop.

Dave punctuated the quiet. 'You know what I heard from Scotty?'

Scotty was one of the two roving district policemen.

'Did you know Rawlings crashed his car not long back?' The men all nodded, only half interested.

'He told Scotty he swerved to miss a sheep then lost control, but from what I heard it was his missus.'

'Who?'

'His girlfriend. She was doing something, down there . . . so he couldn't think straight. She told Scotty what she'd been doing while she was under the medication.'

The men all broke into broad smiles.

'That poor woman,' said Flynn. 'Imagine having to put up with him all the time.'

Just then Donny stopped his rocking, opened his eyes and picked up his glass like nothing had happened.

'Anyway,' he said, 'Rawlings is probably just going to say you need negative gearing or something.

Sean chuckled with disbelief that Donny had regained composure so quickly.

Millvan smiled. Flynn leant across and slapped him on the knee. 'Anyway, mate,' he said, 'if you need a hand any time soon, we'll help you, won't we Donny?'

'Too right we will,' said Donny calmly.

Dave nodded along with them. 'Will and I can help too, Millvan.' He prodded his brother, but he had finally nodded off.

'Thanks boys.'

'That's what mates are for,' said Flynn.

Millvan didn't know how to thank him so he got up and shook his hand and patted him on the back a few times. Then he shook Donny's hand and then Dave's. He didn't shake Sean's hand because he hadn't offered him anything.

'Hell, if things are that bad I'll have to cash my cheque before you get to the bank, hey,' said Sean.

'Don't you worry,' said Millvan.

Flynn looked pleased with himself. He'd done what he'd come to do and it sobered him a little. He looked at Dave and tipped out his glass. 'You better get this one home, hey Dave,' he said, motioning towards Will.

'Yeah, it's about that time,' said Dave. 'Time for bed.'

They got up, picked up the eskies and walked slowly

back to the house. Away from the fire they found the night had got much cooler; the moon had moved so that the roofs didn't reflect moonlight any more. When they got closer to the house they saw the trees were like big black figurines against the horizon. Some looked like huge round faces and one was tall and long like a horse's head. Millvan found that if he looked at the smaller shapes for long enough they dissolved the same way stars do.

It was lights out and even though Millvan was drunk, there was an image that formed just before he went to sleep. It was the view of a house from a valley. It was alone on a hill. He couldn't formulate a garden or other details but he knew the house was white and there was a shed full of fishing poles and crab pots. He knew it had an encircling verandah, was set up on stumps and you could taste the Pacific on a sea breeze that smelt of fishing. Sometimes he saw its distant blue shimmer but mostly the image was just of the house and valley. The valley was full of trees save for a few fenced-off paddocks running down the back of the hill. Some of the trees were fruit trees. The paddocks had a few cattle in them. Millvan didn't get to see any more. He was asleep. It was an image he'd fallen asleep to a lot lately, ever since the drought had begun.

Millvan lay awake in the early morning dark. Outside the window the figurines he'd seen the night before were just peppercorns again. He could see the top of the big box tree as he lay in bed. It was the same tree he'd looked at every morning since he'd taken the place on. Its leaves held the night in much longer than the buffel grass. They had a stillness about them. You couldn't see the breeze hit anything but the thick shadows. The grass already had a white tickle on it from the first touch of sun. A Willie wagtail was the first one to sing and then the laughing kookaburra woke the cockatoos and it was morning.

He got up without disturbing Michelle and went and checked on Murray. He was sleeping on one side. Millvan watched his chest move up and down for a moment before shutting his door quietly.

After the usual things he took his coffee and sat for a while on the steps. The breeze blew in and dried his face, wet from the washbowl. Some finches were hopping through the fence playing some game. It was still too early for the others. Their boots stood by the door to the verandah. He was thinking about the bank and maybe getting in loggers when a humming started beneath his leg and a mud wasp flew out. It was one of those big orange ones.

'Why do you have to live there?' he asked of it.

Just then a dog coughed from the gullet and was sick on the lawn. Millvan leant forward to yell the dog away but the wasp, perhaps sensing his anger, buzzed close in retaliation. Millvan stiffened. The sting could make you weep and a bite on the throat was lethal. He slit his eyes to watch it go.

'Why do you have to live there?' he asked it again. 'Live in the trees where *we* don't go when you're hung-over.' He yawned. Today is going to be like that dirty dog, he thought. It's going to sick up something rotten on my lawn.

The dog coughed again and Millvan saw it was Rouger. He looked down at the bile stain on the dead grass. The dog had probably got hungry in the night and eaten some dead thing or a toad. 'Did I forget to feed you?' he asked. Rouger would only get stuck into a carcass when he was hungry. Normally he just rolled in one. Was there a chance he hadn't fed him? 'I fed the bloody dog,' Millvan said aloud. 'I always feed the damn thing.' He caught himself cursing the dingo in the dog, cursed aloud so Rouger came over because he heard Millvan talking. Rouger sat there panting through a tight respectful grin.

'Today I have to go to the bank,' he told the dog.

Rouger smiled at him and edged a little closer.

'I have to go in there and take it on the chin. Take it all square on the chin from Rawlings. Maybe hear I have to sell up . . .'

He stopped and for a long time he thought about that possibility. It had got him up early and stung worse than any wasp.

Rouger smiled again. Millvan watched him.

'Maybe tomorrow I'll have to shoot you, dingo.'

Rouger wagged his tail. He liked being talked to by his master. He came a little closer.

'If I can afford the bullet . . .'

Rouger seemed to think it was all very good. He smiled and rested his head on Millvan's knee.

'Never tame a dingo. You're stupid for trying. You just ran away again, didn't you, and ate more than you could stomach. Serves you right, you were fed well enough. Eat some grass,' Millvan told the dog, patting him lightly on the muzzle. The small moment of contact brought on silence and Millvan looked to the dry sky again for several minutes.

'But you're a good boy aren't you?'

They sat there looking at each other for a while longer till there was some noise in the house.

'If there's unchecked things in your blood you can't help but feel a certain way about carrion,' whispered Millvan.

The dingo yawned stinking breath and Millvan jerked away from him.

'But Jesus, who wants a brown dog barking at his back door?' He pushed the dog's stinking muzzle away and walked up the stairs. He made a quick breakfast and poured another cup of strong coffee.

Later on the others came out drinking their coffee.

'How's it goin'?' asked Donny seedily.

'Orr, *Orrrr* Christ.' It was Flynn.

'You lot look sorrier than the bloody dog,' Millvan told them.

'I got soused,' Flynn complained.

'Your teeth are probably still floating, you useless drunk,' said Donny.

Millvan looked up at the sky as they carried it on.

Something was different from the day before; the easterly was slighter and the cirri seemed very high, but he couldn't tell exactly what it was.

Michelle came out onto the verandah as he turned to take his cup inside.

'Murray seems to have slept all right,' she said.

'How's his shoulder?'

'I think he may have dislocated it, otherwise it's his collarbone. I'll take him to the doctor later on this morning if it's no better when he gets out of bed.'

He nodded.

'Can you get Terry to shoot a roo for the dogs?' he asked her.

She nodded back at him.

'I don't think they've got any dog biscuits left and I won't get home till late.'

He followed her into the kitchen. Donny and Flynn were sunning themselves on the steps. Flynn had called Rouger over and was patting him. Terry came out and was showing Donny his new skinning knife, running his little thumb over the edge. Millvan saw Donny talking to Terry about something as he walked through the kitchen door.

'Last night they said they'd give us a hand if we need it,' Millvan told Michelle.

'I hoped they would,' she said smiling. 'So if Rawlings wants the instalments from the end of last year you'll just have to ask him for more time. That way we can make use of their help.'

'You're a clever one,' he said before kissing her quickly. 'And I promise we'll be all right.'

She agreed worriedly and gave him a quick kiss back.

'I need you to get us some things when you're in town too,' she said. 'Here's my list, and don't forget to go see Carine for some oil.'

A little time later he said goodbye to everybody and got into his ute. Donny and Flynn got into Donny's ute and followed him out along the drive but then he turned off on the road towards town and they turned the other way. The dogs barked as they drove off.

He got into town early. It was a flat railroad town built around its sale yards, trains and silos. There were gums down the dividing strip, a wooden bridge over a thin river and fourteen pubs in all. The people were descendants of squatters and farmers. On any given day you could see cow cockies, bushwhackers, Aborigines and shooters down the main drag. He walked down to the bakery so the time would go quicker. Someone with a handlebar moustache called out to him. It was Jacko from the newsagency and Golden Casket. He'd owned a farm once.

'Christ you look seedy,' he said. 'Any more rain out there?'

Millvan shook his head. 'How's business in this one-horse city?'

'I may as well have killed that horse,' said Jacko, smiling

and waving some papers he had in his hand. 'I'm just going to bury it.' He pointed to the police station.

Christ knows what he's done this time, thought Millvan. He liked Jacko. He'd lost one of his fingers in an auger but the rest of them were quick as could be. They were always getting into places they shouldn't.

'How so?' Millvan asked.

Jacko ignored him. 'What are you doing here?'

Millvan shaded his eyes and pointed to the shiny building halfway down the street.

Jacko nodded. 'Do you want to drop by later on and the missus will whip us up some lunch?'

'No I can't,' Millvan said. 'I don't think I'll be done before then.'

'True?'

Millvan nodded and couldn't help glancing sheepishly at the bank again.

'I thought you cockies were having a hell of a season?'

'It *was* a hell of season.'

'Well what the *hell* does he want you for then?'

'Probably nothing.'

'You'll be able to make lunch then!'

'Nah,' said Millvan. 'Let's save it for a Sunday and do it properly. Thanks though . . .' Halfway through the conversation he'd remembered he'd already arranged lunch with his stock agent, Colin.

'We'll catch some fish together and have a barbecue,' said Millvan.

'You catch the fish. I'll just drink the beer.'

'We'll do it at your place then.'

Before he walked off, Jacko told him to drop in and get a free lottery ticket if it turned out bad.

Millvan waved the idea away as if it was a blowfly.

He walked over to the bakery and bought a pie to hold off lunch. He looked at his watch, there was still plenty of time before his meeting. He walked to the river and dropped pastry into the current. The pastry sunk before he had a chance to see if any fish came. He crossed the bridge and remembered he had to get some oil from Carine. Carine was one of Michelle's friends who ran a little country kitchen not far from the main street. Her husband pressed the oil. He walked into her store, chatted with her for a while and ordered the oil for later that afternoon.

'How's Phil treating you?' he asked.

'Not so bad,' she said. 'How is Terry, the little tiger?' She always asked after the boy.

'He's still a handful.'

Millvan signed the invoice then headed back up towards the main street. He took the long way past the post office and through a side street with a gun store in it. He paused a moment to look at the pocket knives in the window. He needed a new knife, something to peel his oranges with. By the time he got to the bank he was thinking about fruit picking, imagining the fruit trees that would be by the driveway to the white house on the hill.

Suddenly he looked up at and found the bank was in front of him. He felt as though a hand had reached into his pants and clenched everything together. In a way he felt scared even, like before a rodeo. Then he was queuing to ask for Rawlings.

He was still being gripped by the time he got to the front desk.

He was greeted by a young man. 'How are you today, sir?'

Millvan had just wanted to tell him he was there to see Rawlings but the young man was more interested in reciting the benefits of one of the bank's latest products. Millvan'd never seen this young fella before and didn't listen to him, just looked at his watch and saw he was late. It made him even more anxious. It made him feel vague to look about this place. He needed his wits about him. He was telling himself to keep his wits when he finally got a chance to slip in the details of his appointment. The young man told him to wait for Mr Rawlings.

'And have a good day,' added the young man.

Mindless, thought Millvan as he walked to Rawlings's room to sit down. Rawlings was not there and he sat himself uneasily in the customer's chair.

It was a clinical white room. Even the windowpane had been painted white so you could hardy see out. A big gum tree outside was just a faint grey outline.

I've got to keep my wits about me.

Heavy footsteps sounded down the hall.

Tell him what you think about the interest and keep your wits about you. He's got you by the balls remember.

Finally in came Rawlings with a half-eaten piece of cake.

'How did the harvest go, you old cocky?'

He was very jovial and it made Millvan suspicious.

'Not bad,' he told him. 'A bit early to tell. Shall we get down to it?'

The banker shrugged this off.

'How many acres did you pull off? Must be stubble everywhere. I remember last year we shot twelve good boars off the stubble over on Willy Gumby's place . . .'

Millvan knew what he was getting at now.

'I bet it was a crop all right. I've heard! Too much trash for the headers, thrashing grain out the back . . . Be pigs everywhere, hey?'

'Sorry mate, I've got two blokes that shoot on the place already,' said Millvan.

Rawlings liked hunting with a .243 and always talked about how he reloaded his own bullets. He was pretty keen. The type of keen that makes a man leave gates open in the heat of the hunt. Millvan didn't want him letting stock out all over Arbour.

'How about roos then?' he asked.

'Well there's not so many around . . . Maybe next winter if they come in from the west.'

'Sounds great. I've got a new scope that'd be perfect.'

Millvan just nodded and Rawlings must have realised he wasn't serious. It made him get professional. He cleared his throat.

'We've conducted a review of the farm. I did a lot of work on possible variables and instalments.'

Millvan was looking at him dubiously with one eye a little bit shut. The banker saw. He tried to use fitting vocabulary.

'What I'm saying is we can extend what's overdue but it's not going to be easy for you. We'd be taking a huge risk.'

'I'll be paying for it no doubt?'

'Well it's not so easy . . . you haven't paid it . . .'

'It's been six bad years up to the good season.'

'Well I know you'll pay it back eventually but we need it now.'

'Who? You and the young fella sayin' g'day at the desk? Surely we can agree to something halfway.'

'No it's—'

'Wouldn't I get six years to pay it back?'

'Yes, we're willing to extend some of the payments.' The banker was moving around a lot in his chair. It made the floorboards creak. He was a heavy man.

'It's the interest,' he said. 'With the interest we'll require on such a risky investment you'd be taking a huge risk to go with it.'

'What else can I do?' Millvan had budgeted on six years to pay it back.

'Sell up,' said Rawlings.

There, he got it. Square on the chin. Bang! and then quiet like when you dive into a pool.

The fat banker was riffling around for the papers. Millvan sat there with eyes that didn't see. He was carried away with the shock and only came back after Rawlings shook the papers he was holding out in front of him. The shock was replaced by a sick feeling.

'Do I have to sell the place?' he asked in disbelief. His whole being stretched towards the banker, every nerve feeling for a response.

Rawlings suddenly felt uncomfortable. He could see the man's eyes. They were very blue and he realised he was staring into them and being quiet and was quite possibly making it worse for Millvan, who seemed to be hanging on the pause.

'No,' he said with genuine sympathy, 'let's not put the cart in front of the horse.' He gathered himself and slowly pushed the air under his palms flat onto the desk. 'It's going to be very hard and very complicated though,' he said carefully. 'And even after the hard part there'll *still* be a very good chance you'll lose Arbour.'

'But how the hell have we got so drastic all of a sudden?'

Rawlings sighed. He knew there wasn't much he could say that would make any sense to Millvan.

'Did you see that program about natural disasters on the ABC the other night?' he asked. Millvan shook his head numbly. Rawlings cleared his throat again. 'There was Cyclone Tracy, Ash Wednesday, locust plagues . . . but no droughts.'

Millvan couldn't answer.

'They talked about people suffering a freak storm and cleaning up the tin and split palms after a cyclone, but not a word was mentioned about drought. By rights we shouldn't be farming this rotten country,' said Rawlings softly. 'It's too dry. But everyone knew that before they got here. Their eyes were wide open. It's not like when a storm comes and lifts up your roof one night. Droughts don't happen overnight, as you know only too well.'

Millvan was still silent but Rawlings continued with his logic.

'A drought takes years and people knew it before they got here so droughts don't make it onto TV.'

'I know droughts,' whispered Millvan.

'Too right,' said Rawlings. He wanted Millvan to see the financial man's perspective on droughts was no different from your everyday Joe's, that Australians accepted the risk of a drought more readily than a cyclone or other natural disasters because the country itself was naturally dry. 'It's nobody's fault the country's stayed dry.' Rawlings talked on about how Cyclone Tracy arrived unannounced on Christmas Eve. Yes, Millvan remembered it. Yes, he remembered Ash Wednesday just showing up too. No he didn't know the thick smoke that engulfed Melbourne for three days was so fine it got into a number of watches and stopped time altogether. 'Oh yes, it got into the tiniest places,' said Rawlings.

'I'm not going to leave,' said Millvan suddenly.

'I hope you don't have to either,' said Rawlings. 'Listen, today I'm just giving you options is all, because that's legally what I'm obliged to do.' He mentioned the figure Millvan would be left with if he had to sell. It wasn't worth a pinch of shit.

Millvan looked him in the eyes and Rawlings grew shifty.

'I'll be damned if I'll leave just like that!' said Millvan. He felt angry all of a sudden. There'd been no forewarning. He was being set up. He was being ripped off. He saw the white house on the hill that he'd dreamt of so often and it made him feel sick. He didn't let himself think of Murray. He was already too angry.

The banker's chair creaked.

'I'll be damned in hell to buggery if I leave at all,' said Millvan.

'No,' said Rawlings apologetically. 'We want to help you pull through it. It's been a tough six years for us too but we are trying to look after you. And it's your turn for a run,' he said. 'Everyone gets a run. When you get a run you'll be in the money.' He said it all very nicely. 'Go out and get yourself a stack of wheat and get another stack of wheat till you've got a great heap of it. Easy hey!'

Millvan was looking at him with one eye half shut again.

Rawlings pushed the papers towards him. 'Anyway, these are what I brought you in to see today.'

When Millvan saw the figures and what he had to pay before the financial year was out, he squeezed his hands together tight under the table. It was much worse than he'd imagined that morning in bed. It made a stress ball in his stomach that felt like a school of catfish. He stared at Rawlings and there was silence.

Rawlings pushed his hands down again slowly. 'That's the only other option we can give you—it's the law.'

'Well it's a buggered law!' Millvan yelled. 'No farmer made a law like that!'

Rawlings didn't know what else to say.

'This can't be right,' seethed Millvan. 'Why didn't you bring me in here earlier to talk about this? You bastards have set me up.'

Rawlings rubbed at one of his eyes with his knuckle. He sighed. 'If you borrow money you pay it back. That's fair.'

'Well if it's so fair, why can't you look me in the eye? I should get six years to pay it back,' said Millvan uselessly. He knew the stone wouldn't bleed and he shouldn't try to push the fat bastard around. It wouldn't do any good. But he wouldn't lie down in front of him either.

The banker watched him. He didn't like this part of the job. He felt like coffee and something more to eat. Why couldn't they understand it was just money? *Don't take it personally*, he thought, *and don't shake hands so hard*. They always leant too close over the desk. He looked back at Millvan rereading everything. He wished he'd just sign. He tried to hurry it along.

'Our solicitor goes on holidays tomorrow and since it's been hard enough getting you here as it is . . .' Rawlings began.

But Millvan was still flicking the pages and couldn't check a long sigh. The banker had heard that sigh many times before and he didn't like it. It always came out of them signing. They sighed like that whenever they signed over the title deeds.

'This is the only time we can do it,' said Rawlings softly.

Millvan nodded.

'We've already spoken with your solicitor at O'Gorman & Grant about it.'

Millvan sighed again and clasped his hands upward under the table. He was thinking and thinking and knew this was the last chance he would get. The bastard had the deeds if the next three years didn't pay for the last six. The dog was throwing him a bone but it had a smell to it. It stunk of interest, and the papers he was talking about meant even if he grew another solid crop of wheat he'd still have to kill interest. He'd need a bloody good crop and a good year after that—it was about time he had a good run. But three years in a row was a bit much. Damn that soft bastard's interest. Interest could grow faster than wheat sometimes. He'd had to kill the bloody stuff off once already. Once when it hadn't rained a decent rain for two years and sheep were living off salt licks and sticks and had to be fed out in the paddocks. He remembered when the pipe bust. It was the middle of summer and he was so busy feeding lambs and welding together his broken hay trailer that he didn't get out to the eastern block for three days. In the paddock were fifteen hundred ewes, all dead. The pipe had bust halfway out to their paddock from the river and they'd died thirsty. He found them piled up on the riverside fence. A few had jumped over from on top of the dead ones into the next paddock and headed upwind but there was no water in that paddock either and they were dead on its fence. They all died snuffing the water in the wind. He had to get up half an hour earlier and work harder for years because of that.

Every day since he'd prayed for those sheep. And he'd made it up. Yeah, he'd killed his fair share of interest all right.

He felt the sweat on his palms and wiped it on his trousers. He looked at his hands and remembered how that time had nearly broken him. When he found those sheep he fell on the ground and kept pounding it hard till he got cut deep above the knuckles.

Rawlings smiled nicely again.

Millvan thought suddenly of what the dog had done that morning. *Didn't I feed him?* he asked himself distractedly. Then he snapped back.

'You asked me before how the wheat went?' said Millvan.

'Yes,' said Rawlings, sensing the angry moment had passed. 'How did it go?'

'It went well, and you know, those blokes who come out shooting may not even be out till after Christmas.'

'Oh really,' said Rawlings slowly, but he kept his eyes on the papers and didn't look up at Millvan.

'Maybe you could come for a shot if you like?' It hurt Millvan to say that but the thought of Murray made him do it. He only wanted to give the place to Murray.

But Rawlings continued to ruffle papers and ignored him. He just wanted to know how much the harvest would make. So they discussed Millvan's best possible projections at great length but in the end Rawlings concluded that the crop wouldn't make much of a difference. It was a conversation of rates and variables, of tactics, and it took up the better part of the encounter and the last of Millvan's hope that Arbour wasn't under serious threat. Halfway through the discussion Rawlings apparently heard a noise outside in the corridor.

'Alice,' he yelled suddenly. 'Come in here would you.' A woman tiptoed in, introduced her presence humbly. 'Take some petty cash and get me a pie from Lawson's would you, love.' She went out immediately.

Finally they resumed the nuts and bolts of the interview without further mention of Millvan's offer to come shooting. Rawlings handed him the pre-prepared documents as he finished his last piece of pie.

'You know I'm going to sign, don't you?' Millvan said in the end.

The banker shifted. His chair made that noise again.

'I wish I could be more ... lenient with you,' he said helplessly, 'but I can't. I really can't. It would've been better for you if the good season hadn't moved the market so fast.'

'The good season,' said Millvan softly. 'You only started sending the notices after the good season got the market moving, and before then you sent me money. What do you honestly suppose a bloke should do?'

The banker shrugged his shoulders and lowered his

eyes. He caught a glimpse of his watch. 'I'm really sorry, Millvan, but I've got to be somewhere fairly soon . . .'

Millvan shook his head, staring Rawlings in the face.

'We're a generous institution,' said Rawlings putting on his coat, 'and we'll try our best to look after you.' He watched Millvan sign the papers and pick himself up.

'Now don't be too late out of town tonight,' he said, 'or you might clean up a roo driving home.'

Millvan put the papers into an envelope.

Rawlings didn't know what else to say and Millvan walked out.

He dropped a copy of the variation agreement in to his accountant and his solicitor before heading to the pub.

Both said not to worry too much. 'You won't lose it.' Hell, he'd get a bill for the time they'd taken to give that useless vote of confidence. It depressed him even more. They didn't know shit. If they were so smart, Rawlings wouldn't have called him in to the bank in the first place.

He had to walk all the way down to the Clarence Hotel. It was on the corner. Heading down he saw a dirty beggar with a sign on the street. He walked past him. Inside the pub he found Colin, his agent, reading the sports page of the paper. The place was full of mirrors and everywhere you looked someone seemed to be staring back at you. Up on the wood was an old drunk yelling out every once in a while. An Aboriginal barman was keeping him quiet.

When Millvan sat down he realised just how tired he was. The anger and the nerves had gone out of him. Now he felt stripped down, hung-over and plain tired.

Colin looked up over his paper at Millvan but didn't put it down.

'I've got a top-notch mob of calves for you in western New South Wales—Santa Gertrudas,' he said, his sharp eyes flicking from Millvan to the paper.

'Oh no, I—'

'You don't want them? I saved them for you.'

'Nah, I don't want 'em.'

'I'll give them to Donny Graw or somebody.'

The drunk yelled out something about the Wallabies to them. He must have seen Colin's sports page.

'I don't care if you give them to Donny,' said Millvan.

Colin looked at him closely then tucked his paper halfway under the tablecloth.

'How was the bank?'

'Could I have some of that paper?' interrupted a man on the adjacent table. He was one of those people who tip their chin up at the end of the sentence.

'What? Do you want a dinner too?' sneered Colin.

'Oh sorry . . . I thought it was the pub's.' His chin tipped again as he turned away.

'Bloody idiot,' muttered Colin. 'Listen, you'll have to tell me if you want these calves . . .'

Just then the waitress came to take their order.

Both ordered steaks.

'I don't want any calves just now,' said Millvan.

The agent wasn't listening.

'. . . Just not now, that's all.'

'Gee the steaks are good here,' said Colin.

'What?'

'They're always good. Listen, I'm seeing Graw later this week, you sure you don't want them?'

'Just not now, mate,' said Millvan.

'Gee these steaks are going to be good.'

'Are they Santa Gertruda steaks?' asked Millvan. Normally he would have bought those calves.

'No, they get their meat through Dougalls—probably Hereford or Angus, the sort that go *under* a fence.'

They ate and it was good and the vegetables were fresh from the morning markets but Millvan forced it, drank a quick beer then told Colin he had to go and do some shopping. The drunk yelled out something like, 'Jacky-Jacky's a little nancy girl' to the barman just as Millvan was leaving.

The barman threw him out.

'He can't handle the lunchtime crowd,' he told Millvan. Millvan grinned thinly.

'But he makes good business of a morning, don't you, cuz?'

'Bright 'n early,' said the drunk.

He was still there on the street when Millvan reached the ute.

The air was stale and dusty in the cab. He was glad he'd had lunch with Colin. It had delayed the immediacy of Rawlings's words. But now they crept back into his mind. To Rawlings Arbour was nothing more than a little word on a page with bank letterhead saying 'default'. The white house on the hill didn't fit on that page and Murray was nowhere in the fine print. That was the set-up. The banks were always allowed to point to their fine print but they never let Millvan point to his. Murray was in Millvan's fine print. He held reservations in fine print for Terry and Michelle too. It made him angry. The white house on the hill was something he ought to be able to point to. It was a shit of a system.

'What a fuck,' he yelled aloud. A woman stared at him as she walked past his ute. He watched her go and then told himself to calm down. He looked down the street and saw the drunk still sitting on the pavement outside the pub. It depressed him.

I probably should have let Colin in on it, he told himself. I might need him on side—*hell, I'll need everybody on side because this is the worst it has ever been.*

He looked at himself in the rear-view mirror. He was grey as the gum through Rawlings's window.

I am old, he told himself, *maybe too old to be getting up earlier and going to sleep later for the sake of interest. I wish I could be at my house by the sea*. He pictured it with glaring sunshine off the whiteboards. The sea was off in the distance. He saw whitecaps and gulls. And so he found himself sitting there with the sea in his head. He saw big waves and cool spray too. He saw himself looking down at it from the white house on the hill. He pictured the sea for a long time but it crashed out when he thought of his family. Arbour was for Murray, and Michelle deserved the white house. Millvan had always seen it like that. It couldn't change now.

Suddenly he felt determination sweep over him as if he'd opened the window to let the air rush in.

It took about four hours to drive home. He'd try to figure out what he was going to do on the way.

Before he set off he went by the Rural Traders to check the price of pine. Afterwards he spent the rest of the afternoon picking up the oil and groceries Michelle had asked for. An hour before dark he pulled the ute out onto the main drag and the town slipped behind him.

Soon he was in the bush again on the narrow little road that was partly surfaced with tar and gravel. The gravel was mined in the red ridge country of the desert. Before too long he saw a road train looming up ahead.

When the road trains went through, the dust would powder the trees rouge like old women's cheeks. Bulldust hangs finer than flour and all those wheels brought it out of the gravel like beating clothes with a stick. It got into your mouth and came up through the air vents and made the dogs cough. He could see it rolling out and fanning into the trees on the road's edge, coming straight for him. He hit it with the sea crashing in his head and the dust in his face. Then he could hardly see and had to slow down. He concentrated on the road for a time and thought of nothing else. Soon the dust settled and it was clear enough to see miles ahead down the straight road. He knew he ought to concentrate on how he was going to make everything all right but when he came to the first bend he was thinking about the little shed full of fishing rods next to his white house. He'd always liked fishing for its calm. It was a time to attach your troubles to a line and drown them in the sea.

He remembered fishing the hole near the southern end of the rabbit fence. The river was sluggish under the shady gums and bugs made ripples downstream from his bob. His bob slapped the water, bob, bob, bob until he felt a yank. When a fish hit, the bob went right underwater. Then he'd leave the bob still because underneath it the fish knew where the bait was. Then the bob would start moving off slowly in one direction and all of a sudden it would disappear and that was when you hooked it and hauled him up quick onto the bank.

Millvan drove on down another long, straight section of highway. Then he saw himself in the mirror again.

How are you going to work your way out of this, old man?

The ute rattled as he thought.

Grow more wheat, he told himself but that was as far as he got. Each time he replayed Rawlings's ultimatum his mind wandered off to thoughts of his house by the sea and he had to reel himself in to think seriously again. Soon he was visualising a photo of a cod Flynn had caught with a crooked pole made from a stick of cane and a champagne cork dangling a rusted hook. The fish was longer than his arm and was so heavy Flynn had to hold it up by the gills with both hands. Millvan saw that house by the sea so clearly now that it was real enough for him to ache. That was the only place he wanted to go when he left Arbour. It had to be by the sea where he could fish. Fishing kept his mind off things. It would stop him wanting to go back to the bush.

One day he would have to leave Arbour, that was for sure, but he would only leave it if Murray was the one taking it over. He loved the place too much for it to be any other way. It had been the home of his father and his grandfather. He missed it after a day away. A good chunk of his heart was in it. Only a custodian with his own blood could take over it. A house by the sea was nothing if Murray didn't get Arbour.

He drove on past haystacks of frosted wheat and sloping rows of lucerne and medic, over pressed white clay watercourses and wooden bridges, and past whippy saplings and painted mailboxes made from twenty-four gallon drums, till he reeled himself in again.

I could use a lottery win, Millvan told himself. *If ever we could use a lucky draw from Jacko's it'd be now.*

The voice in his head laughed at him. Going to Jacko was worse than ringing up the paper and telling them to run a story about how broke you were. Except fewer people found out if it was in the paper. He didn't want everyone to know about it.

The first thing he'd have to do was cut expenditure. No more beer and nothing fancy. Murray would have to get a job on someone else's place to pay his way at ag college. He couldn't pay him for his work on Arbour anymore. Maybe he could ask Flynn's boys to keep an eye out for a job in the Territory. There was always work for stockmen. It was hard work and there was nowhere for them to go of a night time to blow their money. The dogs would have to eat nothing but roo meat, no dog biscuits. He'd have to give them injections for heartworm. And hell, he'd have to work. There'd be no fishing for a while and he wouldn't taste fish again until he caught one himself.

The sun dipped down behind the furthest trees to the start of another long November twilight. He wished he were sitting home right now because he was tired. Hell he was tired. He wished he were home with a beer and the evening to enjoy.

But you can't just drink beer like that any more, he reminded himself, *it's going to be bread and water. A real pious diet, more pious even than Father Lemon.* Father Lemon was the local priest who held sermons in people's homes each week. He liked his grog. Flynn got on well with Father Lemon. They'd been good friends since Flynn's wife had died. Donny spoke with him a lot too. Millvan wasn't that religious but got on with him well enough.

How are we going to beat the interest though, Millvan asked himself.

He heard Rawlings's voice in his head: *Go out and get yourself a stack of wheat and get another stack of wheat till you've got a great heap of it. Easy hey!*

He didn't know how he'd tell Michelle. He worried about it till he saw a wallaby. He watched it cautiously choose the bush and not the last-minute dash in front of the on-coming ute. *I'll just have to tell her*, he told himself. *I'll just say, 'Darling, I know you wanted to get away for Christmas this year but we'll cut a pine sapling instead. There'll be no fish and no beer neither.*

'No, my darling, because it's the worst it has ever been.'

Meanwhile at home Rouger had run away again and Michelle was singing out into the dark for him to come eat a piece of the roo Terry had shot. But Rouger was running through trees that had never known an axe and was too far to hear her.

He was running through olive-green leaves, tough barks and greyed trunks. Swishing grasses opened up for him and the trees watched him go by. He ran through thick clumps of

them in the river block where they stood with a high inter-
twined canopy like lovers stretching out to touch fingertips.
Rouger ran with the voice of the dingo singing over all the
other breeds to the rhythm of his running and what he saw.

The sky on the leaves comin' on silver, the trees and the
leaves movin' the breeze, hushed moon high over it all.

The dingo drowned out the other breeds in him, pushed
them out of him and sent them off home with their tails
curling up under their balls. They left him with the silence of
the moon. He made no noise but was seen anyway. He scared
a bird and sent it off flapping hard at the darkness. It must
have been an owl. Most birds make a squawk but like to stay
put because they cannot see another place to fly to. He scared
a wallaby too and it made one big smack-hop with his tail
then lots of quiet hops as usual. Wallabies put emphasis on
the smack-hop to warn their mates. Rouger ran on through
the tangle and spooked rabbits so they dissolved into holes;
he did not hear them running clean and silent. He was
hunting something always further on. The cornucopia of the
bush was waiting ahead somewhere. Further on he would cut
blood onto the most ancient of tables and the dingo would
eat its fill with the other breeds standing back in respect till
he had finished. Rouger ran on with the rhythm.

The sky on the leaves comin' on silver, the trees and the
leaves movin' the breeze, hushed moon high over it all.

Millvan had gone over the halfway mark now but was exhausted.

I am awake, he told himself. Occasionally he would catch a glimpse of a light way off through the trees. Most places were too far in off the road and the scrub too thick for him to see their lights. The scrub grew close to the road and the headlights did not pierce it. It made the white dividing strips much better to look at.

He didn't look though and reminded himself about the smash if he did. He didn't want to do that again. He couldn't afford another busted ute or another lay-off with a busted leg.

There is another two hours yet, he said to himself, *which is all the better because you haven't thought this through.*

He knew Rawlings was right about needing more wheat. He'd double crop all the paddocks. He'd even put it in the house paddock. And he'd sell the cattle as soon as the market shifted. Hopefully after Christmas it would shift. Then he could ring Colin and get him to sell the cattle. His mind didn't wander now. He calculated how many acres he could put under wheat. Even with the house paddock it wouldn't be enough and he needed three years of good wheat crops. He wouldn't get three good crops if he double cropped for three straight years though. The soil wouldn't support it.

Well I'll chop all the bloody trees down and plant wheat everywhere instead.

But the only trees left were in the river block and he wouldn't cut them down. It would take far too long.

We need more wheat next year though, he said to himself. *We could get a dozer to clear the timber and run it all into cultivation.*

But he knew it was too expensive to rent a dozer and clear land.

'We'll need the wheat though.' He was sure of that now. Good wheat crops would save them. Cattle were no good, a summer crop was too risky but he had plenty of wheat seed.

He pressured himself to think how he could get a dozer and clear.

You can't, he told himself. *You can't even afford a lottery ticket because you've got to save and it's too expensive for you to go fooling with money you don't have because look where it gets you.*

But I need a dozer to clear land.

You ought to worry more about keeping a clear head and staying awake.

But I am awake. It is just because I'm getting hypnotised and because I'm tired.

The straight roads and the white dividing stripes were like a pendulum. The long white seconds slipped by with the tar under the fender. Tick, tick, tick, just the road and the bush beside it to look at. The stress of seeing Rawlings, the drinking the night before and the long harvest had taken it right out of him and there was still an hour of straight roads to go.

He put some music on and it was the scratchy AM station that played the old songs he never got to like. They reminded him of his grandfather.

His grandpa had never cleared out the river block. He used to like all those old trees. It had some pockets of tea-tree and brigalow but mostly it was tall gums and pine. You could get away from a gusty wind in those trees. All of a sudden it made him sad to think of clearing them. All the Kakadu birds nested there when they flew down during the spring. Some even came from Papua New Guinea. He remembered showing them to Michelle and hearing the magpie geese and the whistlers fly over to roost in the evenings. You could set your watch to those ducks.

He knew his grandfather had cut plenty of scrub and would understand if he cleared these trees, but his grandfather had loved it along the river there.

'I cursed the scrub,' he used to say. 'The stuff took forever to chop out and it sprang up just as quickly. I hated the trees from the first chip I split and that means I hated them for two decades because that's how long it took to cut the roads, the front paddock and the fence lines. But it grows around you and over you and after a while you realise you can't cut it all. So you leave it; besides, it shades you when you fish. It's the way of things. That's why I left trees all along the river.'

Millvan liked those old trees too. They had never known an axe. It was pure country. When he walked among them he knew that was how the country must have been thousands of years ago. He stopped himself being senti-mental. *The way of things has changed*, he told himself. The pine that grew in there would fetch a good price. It was a way of combating the interest, which is what he had to do. He wished there was another way to do it though.

'Just the pine because it's the worst it has ever been,' he said aloud.

He caught a glimpse of his face staring haggardly back at him from the mirror.

Just then some roos hopped onto the road out in front of him and he had to time it with the brake to make sure he missed them. They liked to sit on the tar because it held warmth after sundown and they could nibble at the green pluck in the road ditches. They got dumb when they saw the lights.

He didn't want to hit a roo.

He saw the lead go across and then the others went bounding over as one continuous mass—five or six of them. As usual he timed it for the last ones he hadn't seen. They came and he missed them by a couple of lengths.

God he was tired.

The road grew narrow and straight and brigalow pushed closer to it. The headlights glared off the dull olive-green leaves and bounced back full of yellow eyes. Occasionally a big gum would lean right over the road itself. Millvan saw the low new moon through the top of the dash. It fluttered through the big gums and cut a scythe over the brigalow. It was smudged from a light atmosphere drawn over from the east.

The ute crested over a sandy hill. He decided he would cut all the pine. The moon hovered and seemed to fly with the ute. It was there when he got off the asphalt onto the dirt road and it was there when he went past Satang.

I'll take the pine and that way most of the trees stay. Grandpa would've cut more if he knew Dad needed it and I'll cut pine because Murray needs it.

Then he went over the last cattle grid.

I'll take the pine and double crop wheat.

He parked the ute under the peppercorn tree, walked inside and went to bed. He would get to the white house by the sea one day. Rawlings hadn't stopped that just yet.

'I tell you, the pine is the only way,' said Millvan the next morning.

Michelle looked up from the bank papers. Millvan had been poring over the accounts since sparrow's and had barely spoken a word.

'If I take the pine, plant a good summer crop and then get a decent wheat crop next year, we'll hold on for a while.' Michelle nodded but she had a scowl on her face.

'How do they expect us to make money all of a sudden?' she asked angrily and pushed the agreements away from her. 'They give you enough rope to hang yourself,' she said. 'Five years they've been saying we'll help you through, we'll help you through. All along they made sure that we'd default later on.'

Millvan rearranged the bank documents in a pile. 'Donny and Flynn will help,' he said, 'and we'll go back to living like we did after the sheep died.'

'That fat bastard,' said Michelle ignoring him. 'I don't know how he lives with himself.'

'We'll only have to do it till we get a grip on things,' continued Millvan. 'We'll kill our own meat, you and Terry can get a veggie patch growing again, we've got the chooks . . . and some things we'll have to go without.'

Michelle suddenly realised what Millvan was saying. There'd be no fresh fruit, fish or new clothes. She'd have to darn all the socks. And there'd be no brandy. She thought of Rawlings again and swore. 'You fucking arsehole.'

Just then the dogs went off. The cacophony sounded from down the drive and broke the mid morning calm.

Murray yelled from outside, 'MAIL'. He was finishing his assignments at a table on the verandah.

Millvan closed his accounts book and went outside to meet Keithy in the spinning dust. His truck was still hissing and a slow click came from under the windscreen. It had a long tray of hardwood slats piled up with new boxes, sheep dip, drums of oil, some slabs of beer and a few big gas cylinders. Keithy had been doing the mail run for twenty-eight years. Everybody knew him and he always had a joke. He dropped in to have tea with all the ladies and none of the men ever worried because besides the fact he was married and a good fella, he was also just about the ugliest poor bugger ever born.

'Howdy-do-dee,' he said through gapped and broken teeth.

He clapped dust from his old felt hat then adjusted it on his head so the earmark in the felt faced them.

'What d'ya know?' asked Millvan.

They talked for a while about the cricket tests and the

storms supposedly coming down from the Highlands before they went over to the shed.

They unloaded the steel fence posts and batons Millvan had ordered months ago then sat there looking at the peppercorns, slugging on water and wiping at their sweat.

Keithy was looking back towards the house.

'You ought to chop that bloody thing out,' he said.

Millvan looked over at the old box tree in front of his bedroom window.

'That's dead wood. That'll fall and get somebody killed,' Keithy went on. He talked at a hundred miles an hour. 'I've seen it happen too. You ought to chop it out. Remember old Argyle got half his teeth knocked out and broke a collarbone from that one little branch?'

'Yeah I suppose it is getting a bit old,' said Millvan.

'*Old!* The bloody thing's dead.' He spat on the ground and looked at Millvan, shaking his head. 'Go and tell ya mum to put the kettle on and get me a cup of tea whilst I cut that bloody thing out,' he said to Murray, who had just arrived.

Murray walked off with his big heavy bandage, wobbling his head from left to right.

'What the hell happened to him?'

'Cleaned up by a steer.'

'Orr.'

Millvan looked over at the tree; it had his initials engraved into it from God only knows when. He always liked looking into its branches when he was in bed. It was what he woke up to.

'Do you want me to chop it down for you?'

Millvan kicked the ground. 'Nah, not really.'

'I've got McCardle's axe on the back—he sent it in to get a new handle, said it's seen more wood than a tidy beaver. Why don't you chop it out?'

'I don't know,' said Millvan honestly.

'Why not? That's a dangerous lump of wood you've got yourself. If I were a big bird I wouldn't even roost in it.'

'Oh you go on!'

'Nah, true,' he said smiling. 'It stinks dangerous to high heaven, stinks worse than crocodile shit.'

Just then out came Michelle, walking fast and smiling from ear to ear. She liked Keithy and Murray had told her he wanted to cut the old box down.

'God bless you Keithy,' she said.

He whistled at her. She went up to him and gave him a kiss on the cheek. They laughed at each other. Millvan didn't laugh. He looked at the ground.

'I've been trying to get him to cut that ugly thing out for years,' she said. 'Look at the awful thing sticking out on an angle.'

They all looked over at it. It was big, heavy and black-looking with only a few old clumps of long leaves way up the top. The low limbs were grey and had hollowed out. It looked nearly dead all right.

Millvan looked back first at his wife's excited face and then at Keithy skipping back and forth on his toes.

'I'll chop it out for you,' said Keithy, slapping him on the back. 'That way it's not you who did it, see?'

Millvan nodded. 'I suppose it is dangerous.'

'You want to go into Grandpa's block and hack it to pieces and you're worried about this old thing?' Michelle shook her head in disbelief.

'This isn't worth money now is it?' said Millvan.

'But it's ugly.'

'You see,' said Keithy. 'And I get to test out McCardle's axe. I've been thinking about how to do it all morning,' he said, laughing.

Millvan was still looking at the old tree. 'I broke my arm falling out of that damn tree once.'

'The bloody thing,' yelled Keithy from inside the cab of his truck. Then he laughed to himself.

Michelle wandered over to Millvan and said he might want to hook up the gas cylinder now that it was delivered. He went and got a spanner and then had to shimmy under the house on his back to reach at the plugs to screw them in backwards and make them tight.

He heard the big crash as he finished with the gas plugs. He went out to Keithy and saw the tree lying there and the stump all wet, chewy and rough.

'Bit of life in her after all,' said Keithy, rubbing sweat onto the edge. 'But hell, that's no tomahawk.'

Millvan smiled and started walking away. 'Go in and

have a cup of tea,' he yelled over his shoulder. 'I'll see you in a minute.'

'Where are you off to?'

'I've got to let a horse out for a run. I'll be with you in a sec.'

'Righto mate,' yelled Keithy.

Millvan made it almost to the stable and the lucerne-chaff stink was upon him when Keithy started splitting out the hollow trunk. When Millvan got back from the stables he saw it had been split clean in half. The thin leafy branches had been cut off and stacked in a pile under his window.

Swinging McCardle's axe must have taken it out of Keithy because he stayed for some time drinking tea with Michelle.

Millvan opened and shut his account book as he listened to them talk about the races.

'Hear you know the Roggerson fellas pretty well,' interrupted Millvan finally. The Roggerson Logging Crew was based in the same dingy little town as the post office and was the only company anyone ever used to log their pine. They were the only loggers in the shire.

'Orr yeah, Jimmy's me brother-in-law. Do you want to cut all the bloody trees down now, hey? Got a taste for it?'

He was laughing in between talking and looking sharply first at Michelle and then Millvan.

'I thought you had the sulks just then when we cut the old girl down,' he said.

Millvan looked him in the eyes and smiled. 'I want you to get them Roggerson fellas so we can cut a hell of a lot more.'

Keithy was serious all of a sudden. 'I suppose I could ring up later this arvo,' he said tentatively, 'and see what they're up to.'

'That'd be good.'

'Yeah no worries, but you know what the bastards are like?'

'She'll be right.'

'They're a pack of idiots,' he continued. 'The old bloke is mad as a meat axe.'

'He won't come though, will he?'

'The boys aren't any better.'

Keithy tippled at his tea slowly and Michelle refilled his cup.

Millvan sniffed. 'I don't care so long as they're willing to cut and haul pine out of a river block full of it. The sooner they start the better.'

Soon afterwards he left them. He had to check on water and needed the rest of the day to fence off a grass paddock for his heavy bullocks. He loaded up some of the new steel posts Keithy had brought, cut some wire, took the strainers and pliers and then drove off.

Old man Roggerson himself called that night and said he'd send out a crew the next day. Two of them were his sons who Millvan was 'extra lucky to be getting'. The rest were blokes who worked old school and who could 'skin a fucking cat any way you want'.

Be that as it may, the crew didn't show the next day and Millvan wasted nearly the whole day waiting for them. Three days later they set the dogs off when their rig finally rolled over the grid. The dogs barked and barked and some harsh voices yelled at them. Millvan didn't need to see the truck to know it was them. The dogs kept barking till Millvan came out of the house and told them off.

The loggers were dirty men. They had tattoos on their legs and necks and had thick beards. They had beer guts and wore singlets and steel-capped boots. They had an old red truck with a long tray that had a little tractor with hydraulic forks on it. There was an enormous yellow dog chained up under the tractor.

'G'day,' they said and introduced themselves. Millvan shook their hands.

'What news from the great capital?' he asked them. They laughed at the old country piss-take.

'What do you want us to cut?' asked the one who'd made the introductions.

'Pine.'

'Just pine?'

'It's worth money isn't it?'

'What does it matter, our wage is still the same.' He said it bitterly.

'Just pine if it's worth good money,' said Millvan. 'Now let me tell you blokes a few things about where you're working.

'The pine on Arbour,' he began, 'is found in country along the river. You'll come across sheep and cattle . . .'

Immediately he lost their eye contact.

'. . . that are in paddocks you'll have to drive through . . .'

They listened with only half an ear and made jokes amongst themselves as he explained how old the pine was. Millvan then drew a map for them in the dirt to show them where to go.

'There are cattle in those two paddocks as well,' he said, pointing with his boot. They looked at him and then looked back at the dirt map.

'You'd better shut the gates,' said Millvan finally.

They nodded. One of them smirked, 'Bit hard for some people, is it?'

'Yeah, some people,' said Millvan in a light, friendly voice.

'We'll shut your gates, mate. Don't you worry about us.'

Millvan didn't say anything but looked up at their dog.

'You blokes got any guns?'

The one who had spoken first stepped up. 'Guns?' he asked quizzically. 'We're not gunna shoot your trees down.'

'That dog looks like a hunting dog.'

'Mate, don't worry about us.'

'I'm not.'

'Who said we had any guns?'

'Nobody.'

'Well he's Mick's dog.'

'How are you, Mick?' asked Millvan.

Mick didn't say anything. The other one kept talking. 'He's not a hunting dog, are you Bronson? He's a big friendly bugger. I'm sure Mick won't mind if you keep it here and let it play with your kids.'

Mick smiled.

'No, that's all right,' said Millvan. 'Just make sure he doesn't play with my stock.' One of them smirked and the talker kicked out the map. 'Don't you worry about us, mate. We'll get a camp up in the pine and stick to ourselves. We're just gunna chop some wood, hey boys?' They all chuckled at the way he said it.

'That's why you're here,' said Millvan facing up to them, 'but if you've got guns, or if I hear shots—you'll know about it.'

'Is that right?'

'That's right,' said Millvan. The talker had uncrossed his arms and had his head a little to one side. Millvan saw one of them beside him watching on without expression.

'Is that right?'

Millvan just nodded; the logger had come right up so his chin was in his face. One of the others had been fidgeting a little.

'Hey Gary, let's get out and set up camp, mate. C'mon mate.'

Millvan stood there looking at Gary. Gary looked around at them and then faced up to Millvan with his sunburnt noggin.

'You leave us alone, matey, and we'll cut the wood.'

'All right, but no guns.'

'And what are we gunna feed the bloody dog with then?'

Bastards, thought Millvan, but he couldn't do anything with them now. They had a gun and a dog and were sure to run around through his bloody sheep and cattle but he couldn't do anything about them. Getting a ripped shirt and a kick in the guts wouldn't help him get the pine. He *needed* the pine.

'Shoot a roo then,' he said angrily and spat on the ground. 'But if a beast gets shot or one sheep goes missing then none of you get paid.' He turned around and walked back to the house. He heard one of them laugh and then slamming doors and the big yellow dog woofing as they drove away. Millvan yelled his dogs quiet again from the steps.

Michelle put the kettle on when he got inside.

'What's wrong?' she asked. He had a scowl and was muttering under his breath. He didn't want to talk to her about it though.

'Nothing,' he said.

'How were the men? Aren't you going to show them out to the pine?'

'I drew them a map.'

'But don't you think it would have been nicer if you'd—'

He cut her off. 'Just leave it,' he said sternly.

'Are you all right?' she asked.

'Bastards,' he cursed. He stirred in milk and sugar to the coffee. He didn't want to talk about the men to Michelle. She believed all people essentially were good . Millvan didn't want to hear it this time.

'How could you get like that after just five minutes with them?' she asked.

'They're bastards that's all. One of them is a fighter and the others are brainless, boof-head bastards.'

'But after five minutes,' she went on, not wanting to believe it.

'They want to be left alone. That's why they're bastards from the start.'

'What rot! Who would do that?'

'Bastards,' muttered Millvan. He took his coffee and went outside and sat on the steps. There was a big gang of finches squawking at a magpie in the peppercorn.

Moments later Michelle came out and sat close to him on the steps.

'I'll have to take it up to them,' said Millvan.

Michelle didn't say anything. She didn't like fights.

'I don't mean I'll go swinging at them like a pirate,' he said to her before she could protest. 'But I will take it out of their wages if they turn out to be lazy bastards.'

'Yeah, take it out of their wages,' she said.

'They've got a pig dog too, so you can be sure they'll be shooting more than cutting.'

'Well dock them then.'

'Yes but I need the pine. I can take a bit of shit for the pine. At least the bastards are here and I can get back to work.' He slapped on his working Akubra and whistled for Rouger but Rouger did not come. He hadn't seen Rouger for a few days and wondered if the mongrel had run away again.

The storm whipped in just on dark. He could smell it as he drove home with it banging behind him. He saw lightning much further away, in two different places on the touch of the horizon, but he couldn't really see how big it was in the faded dusk. He smelt it as he fed the dogs and he smelt it as he wound up the windows on the ute. Then it rumbled. It was like being up close to a bull in the night. It clapped out lightning and he worked out from the thunder that it was close enough to be above him. A kilometre for every three seconds between the flash and the thunder. This one was right alongside the house and those big anvils covered some territory. It was sure to rain but the corrugated-iron roof lay quiet.

They ate dinner quietly around the wooden table. Everybody thought of the storm and hoped it would hit them. They watched the dark windows for flashes and had an ear turned upwards to the iron. They waited and waited.

Then slap, slap, slap, heavy bloody splats on the roof. It was a good sound. It picked you up in the guts. Everyone was hoping.

'Send it down,' said Michelle. Every storm she said it. She thought it helped it to rain. Everyone had little superstitious things they did when there was a storm around. Millvan went onto the verandah and paced. Murray went out and checked the rain gauge to make sure a hornet hadn't clogged it. He got wet from the big spots.

'Bring it down in bucketfuls,' yelled Michelle.

It dragged out and the wind picked up and that's when Millvan got worried because he wanted it nice and calm to set in and rain well. It sprayed a little then stopped just as quick.

Everyone was strung out. It was still close. It would rain. Big spats kept hitting into the roof. Maybe a quarter of an hour went by like this. Then they started thinking it was going to blow like hell. Pour and blow and crash thunderbolts about the place. Outside it was thrashing the peppercorns and yanking the grass in waves and when it clapped out Boom! they could see everything slivery silver like a darting fish.

A sudden tirade of heavy splats drummed the roof.

'Send it down,' said Michelle again.

But the drumming eased off to a negligible backdrop to the wind.

'Come on,' she yelled, 'you can do it.'

Millvan looked at his wife and it made him think of when he'd taken her away after the wedding. He saw the hotel they'd stayed in by the main beach. There was a lot of sand between the cafe underneath their room and where the sun got up over the water. They swam every morning before breakfast. Then she would get coffee and he would get the papers from the store and they would sit on the balcony and watch the birds chase the whitebait the mackerel had schooled up behind the reef. During the day they went on boats and skied on the river. They drove about the rainforest and lunched on fresh seafood from the trawlers. Sometimes they got drunk. Usually they ate at a restaurant and when they finally got away they would go back to the hotel and make love under the big fans.

'Come on, you can do it,' Michelle yelled again. But it didn't do it and they waited and waited and hoped it'd get a roar up on the iron but it never did.

'It's swung north,' said Millvan finally. That's what the storms had done two years ago and it was bad to think it was the start of something all over again.

'The front could still be behind it.'

Millvan hung his head out the window to look at the sky. It smelt nice.

'There are stars behind it,' he told his wife.

'It could swing back when it gets more to the east.'

'No, it's gone. There'll be another one coming through though. The system doesn't stop till Friday. We could get the tail.'

Millvan sighed and Murray asked if the clouds had gone.

'Yes mate.'

'I thought you said it was going to rain and we'd double crop.'

'It missed,' said Michelle overhearing.

Millvan went back to looking at the dark sky.

Murray left them and went back into the house. Terry followed him. Some drops still hit the roof and it was too dark to see anything outside. He decided to wait on the verandah.

She made coffee for them and they sat together. There was a gecko on the windowpane down under the outside light. Dozens of moths were butting at the globe. Millvan watched the gecko eat them as Michelle topped up his cup. He was thinking how well geckos did out of electricity, just like kangaroos did well out of bore water. The fridge was buzzing and so was the two-way. That electrical sound was always there in the kitchen. The filter coffee tasted thin.

She saw what he was thinking. 'I didn't put as much in.'

'We can't buy this sort of stuff any more,' he said.

'What sort of chances did Rawlings give us?'

Millvan didn't answer.

'How much do we have left?'

He looked and saw a look of fear flash over her face and he realised she'd seen what his eyes couldn't hide.

'I knew it,' she said. She remembered the worry that had made her ring Donny and Flynn during harvest.

Millvan said nothing.

'Can we afford a house?'

'We could get a house maybe in town, like Jacko's.'

'I don't want to live in a railway house.' She breathed out heavily. 'But it'd be better than nothing at all. I don't want to come out with nothing!'

'We won't come out with nothing,' he assured her.

'I don't want to have to put up with a town. I would die.'

'So we'll get it all back here,' said Millvan. 'We will get it back.' He put his arm around her and she looked away at the window. He rubbed her shoulders.

'So we could lose it all,' she said and then she repeated it softly and shook her head.

'Sure we could. That's why we're talking about this.'

'Talking, talking, talking,' she said. She was still looking away.

'Don't you want to talk about it?' he asked. She wouldn't look at him and he wondered if she was crying.

'I don't know . . . Yes, I suppose I do.'

'From what Rawlings told me,' began Millvan, 'if we sold Arbour now we'd have enough money to buy a little apartment in town, but that's not worth a pinch of shit to me. Anyway, it'll be all right if we work it out here.'

'I can't live there,' she decided.

'And I can't either,' he said.

'If the season turns around then so should the financial situation,' she said, pleading. 'It's logic.'

'We'll just stay here,' he said to her. 'I'm not living in some dog box.'

'I'd never live in a dog box,' she said, leaning forward,

and glaring at him. 'There's plenty of time to be in a box when I'm dead.' He saw her eyes were red. 'But at least it'd be *somewhere* though.' He squeezed his arm tighter around her shoulders.

'We need a house,' he said, 'but one by the sea. I want to live by the sea. I dream of our hill and the house with the shed.'

'It's not fair,' she said. 'We're the ones that have had it rough for six years, living with hardly any money, and now *we're* in trouble.'

'It'll be all right,' he said. He didn't know what else to say.

'How the hell will it be all right?' she screamed at him. '*We haven't got a pinch of shit!*'

'Because I'll work harder than I ever have,' he said. 'It'll be all right and we'll have it all again. We'll work hard like we always did and bugger the storm,' he said, waving the air behind him angrily. 'It's not because of a storm or a suit that we'll go. We'll put Murray here and we'll live by the sea and it'll all be like we wanted.'

'But what if it doesn't rain next year?'

'Six years in a row says it'll rain.'

'If it doesn't we'll have nothing.'

'But it has to,' he said exasperated. He moved so he was facing her. 'I don't want to try anywhere else anyway.'

She knew he was explaining the risk they were taking but she didn't want to accept it.

'But I don't want to do this if you don't want to,' he continued.

'I don't care about what I do—if we go . . . if we stay,' she said shakily.

He cut her off. 'What do you think we should do?' he asked assertively. She was trying not to cry and her yellow hair came out of the tidy knot.

'I want to do what you want to do. I want to stay and I want a house and I want to be by the sea. Poor Murray.'

'We'll get there,' he said.

'Tell me how it'll be all right,' she said sobbing. 'Tell me!'

'It'll be all right. There, I just did,' he said smiling.

'Tell me about the place we'll have by the sea. I want you to tell me again, Mil.'

But Millvan didn't—he sat down and looked at the table.

'Tell me, Mil.'

He shook his head slowly.

'Mil?'

'Should I be cutting down those trees?'

'You're not cutting many,' she said. 'But they were Grandpa's and they are pretty.'

'You didn't find my old box pretty.'

'Yes but on the river they're nice. Tell me about our little house by the sea.'

'All right,' he sighed. He took her hands into his own and kissed them.

'What would Grandpa do?'

She shook her head and pulled at his hand.

'All right,' he repeated, 'it's not right by the sea because we're from the land and it's too crowded close to the shore there. We'll be able to smell it on the easterly though. It'll be back in a little and off the road so we're all to ourselves.'

She was watching him with eyes full. She nodded.

'We'll have enough space to have a milker and some sheep but mostly there'll be just rows of fruit trees. We'll plant fruit trees everywhere.'

'You never told me about the trees.'

'We'll have mangos and macadamia nuts and red papayas and avocados. They'll be so heavy with fruit we'll need people to help us pick it all. It's such a nice view looking up into a tree,' he said softly. 'You can't see the sky but sometimes the leaves open and it's like diamonds dropping on you.'

She was really listening now.

'I want to leave the wild stuff to grow down by the creek. I'll leave it wild so you can walk down and have it close in behind you. The canopy will be dark and cicadas and whip birds will crack over the water.'

'Do you think we'll be able to grow them all?' she asked, smiling.

'Of course my darling.'

She gave a short laugh and wiped at her nose and sniffed.

'We'll get a good pick all year even if the bats come in because we'll blow up wine casks and hang them in the trees.'

'I feel like a wine right now,' she said.

'Well I'll uncork a bottle. Hell, we should have uncorked one after that bloody storm missed.' He got up to get it.

'No, no, no wait,' she said grabbing at his sleeve. 'I want to hear what else.'

He wanted to get the wine.

'Please, please, please tell me what else!' Some new tears ran down her cheek.

He sat back down. 'Well of course there are hills and a little creek. The house will be at the top of the hill to catch the breeze. We'll run a few troughs off the creek for the sheep and then,' he paused to think, 'up on the hill there'll be hoop pines. Big ones!'

'And will there be figs?' she asked.

'Down by the drive.'

'They're the most beautiful trees.'

'Can I get the wine now,' he asked?

'Yes, go,' she said laughing. 'Quick smart or I'll start crying again.' He squeezed her hand hard before he left.

That night as he lay in his bed he realised he would have to work harder than when he was a young man and had cut his knuckles, and harder than in the drought. He went to sleep knowing he would do it too. There were no doubts any more. He was old but after promising Michelle that it'd be all right, the image of the house by the sea was vivid and clear. He listened to her breathing beside him as he fell asleep.

He woke that Sunday with thoughts of work that didn't leave him. They stayed in his hands and it was their will that swung him on. He got up before the sun and started work as it crept up like a drunk's lazy eye. It was too red to look at.

He'd make time. If things weren't done it wouldn't be because of time. There was time. He still had to get ground ready for the summer crop. If the tail of the system came through he wanted to plant straightaway. The ground had to be ready and the logs had to be taken to the mill.

He had to saddle up the planter, inoculate seed and move sheep off the cultivation so when the rain came through he'd be ready.

The water bottle had a dent in it by the time he'd finished half of the job and he was hungry. He decided to take lunch early. He'd taken a portion of corned beef roll wrapped in aluminum paper, four slices of thick bread, a tomato, some relish and bean sprouts. He made good sandwiches and then cut a long spiralling peel off a navel orange with his pocket-knife and ate the quarters. It was fresh and was better than the water. After lunch he started getting sore in the joints of his shoulders and down the bottom of his back.

Every so often he looked around and thought how he loved Arbour.

He remembered the evenings before he was married, when the way the sky looked was important and he wished there had been someone to share it with. There was a copious intensity being young. Now it was different because there were only two colours in his head and he had a wife and children who were greater than the sky and he was older. That was all. He was older now and knew nothing of tomorrow save the way it ought to be. Time was only patience and planning and none of the doors had tigers behind them any more and that was good. It was good to be old, he thought. Giving it to the boy was what it was all about.

You ought to put your back into it some more, he told himself, *and stop thinking. You think too much for someone with so many acres to work.*

So he worked but as he did he thought about how men let themselves be boys again when they swam in the surf. They fooled about in the waves and laughed when they got dumped and he knew that without his Arbour he couldn't be the boy.

I am old but here is where I enjoy my work and it is cleansing. He laughed with his eyes when he saw how dirty he was. *But I'm clear in the head*, he thought. *You need dirt to clear your head.*

Tighten those nuts, he told himself, *or you'll live like one. Sweating rids the pain of the work*, he thought. *It is the work I love the most. I was born for it.* He thought about working on someone else's place but it wouldn't be for Murray or Terry. Everything was for them. That meant the most to him. In his mind he'd always said it was about giving it to Murray but it was for Terry too. He thought of his grandfather and his father and then the boys again. They would have sons one day. He looked around again as he threw away another rusted bolt.

And it's about going to the sea. I can't go anywhere else.

I wouldn't love it and I would die like a man and not a boy. You've got to live with the boy in you.

That is where the dream came from and if you don't have the dream then you die and leave nothing behind.

He remembered all the times he was the boy. All those times it rained and they took the big nets and put them across the swollen creek and took home cod and ate the thick barbecued fillets, or when everyone played tennis together at Guther's. He had a court of termite base. The balls would get red fur and afterwards when you'd sweat wet through there'd be nice sandwiches and the men stood at his bar and talked about cricket and farming. Then there were the rodeos—saddle broncs and bull riding. He'd ridden and had a good mind for talking with the blokes on the circuit and they'd always have a drink afterwards. One time they all got into a big fight with the locals. It started over a woman. She'd yelled out something that the rodeo boys didn't like and because she wasn't much she got told her place. Then it started because her man was there and he was already drunk and the locals all worried the cowboys would break the bar over him or something so they told them to leave. But if you've got sore riding for next to no pay you want a drink, so it was a big fight where everything got broken. Chairs, windows and a lot of faces. Millvan fought for the rodeo crowd. It had gone on for an hour before the police arrived but by that time a woman had yelled, 'They're coming, they're coming,' and everyone had got out of there. Millvan didn't want to be around when the police showed up. They only ever listened to the locals. So the rodeo lot shot through before they could do anything about it. That was a good rodeo. They'd all driven to the next town and drank there. No one followed after you. If you got hunted people could expect trouble and the locals must have thought they'd seen plenty enough already.

Yes, it's all about the boy.

When I go will be when Murray can dream for himself.

Millvan heard the shots early that morning as he finished inoculating the first of many hessian bags of seed. The booms hung in the air as they do only when the calibre is big enough to split hardwood. He wanted the seed ready in case it rained out of the tail of the weather system that was supposed to be moving through that evening.

'God damn them,' he yelled as he stomped down the kitchen stairs.

'Go easy, love,' said Michelle, following. 'Don't start swinging at them or you'll have no pine at all.'

'Those bastards! With them shooting all morning, no wonder Rouger won't respond to a whistle. I haven't seen the bloody dog in two days.'

'Just keep your head.'

'I will,' he muttered, 'but if they've shot my dog ...' He paused and then walked to his motorbike. 'Those bastards shouldn't be shooting.'

She shook her head and then walked back into the shade of the peppercorn.

'You blokes doing a bit of shooting this morning?'

At first they didn't answer.

He saw a dozen or so skins pegged out drying behind the truck and further afield lay the carcasses in a heap under a tree. They were pink like big rats. *If they've shot my dog*, he thought, *I'll fucking* ...

'Looks like you've shot enough to feed your dog already, hey,' he said with control.

'Yeah, you didn't tell us there were so many roos hopping around.' Gary seemed happy and didn't act as though anything was the matter. '*Seven bucks* a skin,' he said. 'We got nine already this morning!'

'I said a roo for your dog,' said Millvan, 'and you said you were going to cut pine if I left you alone.'

'Well Bronson's a bloody big dog.'

Millvan shook his head. 'There's a bloody big difference between shooting one roo and driving around shooting up my country.'

'Orr mate! You want these roos? Skins are worth seven bucks a pop and you rich cockies let 'em jump around.' He had gone sour. 'We're not making seven bucks a bloody tree.'

'I suppose that's why you cut the sandalwood? I told you not to cut that.'

'You said take what's worth money.'

Millvan kicked at the dirt and looked around him; he could smell the nice little logs. Meanwhile Gary had his arms clasped behind his hips.

'What's a few roos to you?'

'You're not here to shoot roos,' said Millvan.

'It wasn't like we went behind your back—you knew we had a dog. Bronson eats one a day and we pot them from the breakfast table. We're not working twenty-four hours a day you know.'

'Well go fishing in your spare time.'

'We aren't doing anything behind anyone's back.'

'If you'd wanted to shoot I might have let you but you're not here to shoot roos and if I'm going to be ducking bullets on my own place I want to know about it.'

Gary smirked and chewed on a stick of spinifex.

'And drag them carcasses away a bit, they'll stink,' said Millvan.

Gary swung his head casually over to them and then looked back at Millvan. His eyes burnt into his face.

Millvan looked around and saw another one looking at him with the same eyes. In one sweeping glance he saw the dog standing tall and panting through yellow canines, little ripples on the water, and distant black storm clouds that looked fat with rain.

'What stinks to you is worth a hell of a lot to us,' Gary seethed.

Millvan saw the others nodding with hateful eyes.

'And a bullet wouldn't pass through these trees, you finicky prick.'

He had his arms down by his sides.

'This pine is worth more than you could believe,' said Millvan.

Gary laughed at him in the face and Millvan walked away. He heard Gary spit.

'No more shooting with a gun like that,' said Millvan over his shoulder, 'and if you're not careful you won't get paid at all.'

He heard one of them say, Jew cocky something or

rather and Gary laughed but Millvan didn't look around till he got to his ute. He knew the bastards' game now. They thought he was a rich fella. They didn't know shit.

He grabbed his axe off the back of the ute. He saw Gary was watching him. He held it up and tested its edge then he walked back over to them.

Gary didn't say anything but grinned and watched him. When Millvan got over to them, he dropped the axe between them.

They watched him silently.

'What's this job worth to you?'

Gary shook his head.

'C'mon, give me a figure.'

'One thing you cockies forget,' said Gary menacingly, 'is what it's like to be scrounging for a buck.'

'If you're scrounging so hard,' said Millvan, 'show me how much this job is worth to you. Now get yourself an axe because we're going to need two.'

One of the others brought over an axe with a red handle. Gary snatched it from him then met Millvan's eyes.

Two of the loggers started laughing. 'Easy on, mate.'

'No,' said Millvan, 'if money is what you're on about then we'll chop some wood together. If in five minutes this old fella cuts more than you then there'll be no more shooting because you won't have worked hard enough. And anyway, if I think you haven't worked hard enough then you can piss off.'

'Fuck off,' said Gary. He dropped his axe down onto the

ground on top of Millvan's. 'I'm not in the fucking mood.'

Millvan scorned him. 'You're not willing to work, are you mate? All you want to do here is piss about and shoot my animals.'

'What?'

'You shot my fucking dog . . .'

'I didn't shoot your fucking dog.'

Millvan looked around at their eyes to see if they were lying.

Gary laughed. His friends were standing stiffly now and looking on with steady eyes as if they knew what was coming.

'Well actually,' said Gary, 'we did have a pot shot at something slinking around the camp this morning. What colour was it, Mick?'

'Red,' he said gruffly, 'like a big dingo.'

'I didn't hear the thump though,' said Gary smiling. 'But you know how it is with a big rifle; sometimes you don't hear the bullet's report—'

Millvan swung his fist at him before he had finished. It connected with Gary's temple and went cross-eyed as he swung back.

Millvan took most of it on the shoulder and straightened to give Gary two very quick punches to the head. They stunned him. It was a good straight left but the right was just off balance and didn't land as heavy as he'd hoped, so Gary didn't go down, just stared back with a numbed expression and maybe took a step backwards. Millvan had time to hit him once more before another bloke came from the side and tackled him. He fell hard and Gary ran in swearing and gave him half-a-dozen or so short pumping rights about the face.

Millvan got an arm in the way of some of them but a couple went through before the others pulled Gary off. Millvan could tell blood was coming from somewhere but he didn't want to wipe at it and sat there breathing heavily whilst Gary struggled against being held.

'Fuck off,' he was yelling. 'Fuck off before I kill you.'

Millvan saw where his right had glanced off and the knuckles had gripped. It had made a good cut under Gary's eye. The men holding Millvan let him go and told him to fuck off quick. He went without thinking to the ute and had started the ignition before the pain set in. He saw in the rear-view that his eye was bloody and there were two good cuts on his jaw and forehead.

As he drove off Millvan saw Gary pick up an axe and hurtle it after the ute.

An hour later the loggers cleared out. Millvan heard the barking dogs and the slow rumble of the truck going past the house. The dogs went with them till he heard the jolting rattle of the truck going over the cattle grid. Then there was no more barking.

He'd expected this. Now the pine would have to be hauled and loaded. Damn those bastards. They hadn't cut the half of it. He'd have to set it into stacked lots himself, ready for when the trucks came to collect it. He'd have to work it all out as he planted the summer crop. Michelle hadn't said anything when she'd tended to his cuts and he was glad. He wasn't sure what to do at all. He couldn't kill the interest with only half of the pine so it all came down to a good summer crop now, and the tail of the weather system wasn't looking too promising. He could plant the summer crop late but then he'd be harvesting it when he should be planting the wheat. The wheat was the most important of all.

Sometime near the end of lunch the dogs sounded again. It was Keithy back on his last run for the week.

He came in quietly. After he'd looked over Millvan's face he explained that he'd met the Roggerson boys on the road. He'd passed them and hooted. Then they'd stopped on the road and talked, the two trucks side by side till another car came along.

'I told old Donny Graw about it,' said Keithy. 'Hell he looked wild, said he'd be down later on.' Keithy peered at Millvan hunched at the table, peered at his face.

'Hey, you're not too bad! Ol' Gary mate said he sorted you out but you're not so bad. I thought you'd be a hell of a lot worse. I've seen plenty come off worse than you.'

'I don't feel like I'm *not too bad*. I can't eat with this jaw.'

'You've still got more teeth than me.'

Millvan smiled.

Keithy didn't stay long though; he seemed bent on leaving and wouldn't have any tea. Michelle asked him to stay but Millvan drank his coffee and let him go. Before long Keithy's diesel truck had faded away to a mosquito hum. Millvan slapped at a bug on his arm.

That night they came around to pick up Murray and see if Millvan was all right. Flynn was putting Murray on a bus to the Territory when he went to town early the next morning. It saved Millvan or Michelle the drive.

'Jeez mate,' yelled Donny as he came through the door, 'they've pushed your can in.'

'I'll be all right,' said Millvan.

Flynn and Father Lemon came in behind him smelling of rum. Father Lemon was bearded and stocky. He held his head tilted upwards when he spoke and was always up for a drink.

'Fuck, mate,' said Flynn. Millvan could see him getting angry.

'Don't worry about it.'

Flynn kept staring. Millvan brought his hand and touched where it was sore on his lip.

'Was it one on one?' asked Flynn.

'Yeah, it was one on one till they tackled me.' Flynn made a spitting noise with sharp air coming over his lips. Millvan patted his high shoulder. 'Fuck 'em, mate,' he said.

Father Lemon pushed past Flynn. 'Don't sink to their level, Flynn.'

But Flynn was seething. 'We ought to go and show them how to count one on one.'

Donny tactfully changed the subject. 'We've come on a rain dance.'

He handed Millvan his empty beer bottle. 'I bought him to make it rain more,' he said, slapping Father Lemon on the back. 'Tonight is your night, old man. We'll bring the storm to you.'

Father Lemon gave a half-smile and so did Millvan.

'I've got a few stitches but I don't need a priest just yet,' said Millvan, touching his face gingerly.

Father Lemon half-smiled again and stared at Millvan's bruised face. 'We know you can't eat but can you drink?'

'We only ask five minutes of dancing,' continued Donny, 'for every fifty points of rain.' They all knew the tail of the weather system was coming through that night. They all hoped to get a hit.

'What if it doesn't rain?' asked Michelle dubiously from across the hall.

'Of course it will,' poked Donny, 'but the key to a rain dance is having a good time.'

'That's right,' added Father Lemon. He was red under the kitchen light.

'Wouldn't be much point to it otherwise,' she said sarcastically.

'We'll bring in the storms,' said Donny, 'but as I said the key is having a good time. What sort of room do you have left in the fridge?'

'What's a rain dance?' asked Terry. He'd joined the men around the kitchen table but Flynn spoke straight over the top of him. He was still angry. 'Is your dog all right then?'

'They didn't shoot it,' said Millvan. 'They wouldn't have been able to resist gloating if they had. The bloody thing has just run away is all.'

'If they did I would have got in my ute . . .'

'Settle,' broke in Father Lemon. 'The man said forget about them. So we're going to forget about them, all right?'

'Yeah yeah,' said Flynn. 'Now I'll have to help you finish cutting the pine . . . finish off that botched job.'

'What's a rain dance?' asked Terry again, louder this time.

Donny looked down at him. 'It's what brings storm heads. But it only works if everyone who is doing it imagines there are raindrops coming down.'

'How do you do that?' asked Terry sceptically. He didn't buy it for a second. Older people always tried to tell him stuff that wasn't true, Donny especially. Donny always did it and he was the last one who ought to be doing it because he was a nutter sometimes when he got drunk.

'Well,' said Donny slowly, thinking, 'you close your eyes and concentrate on the drop flinging away from the cloud —that's the hardest part—but then you just follow it all the way down and that's all there is to it.'

'Yeah sure,' Terry said incredulously.

Flynn spoke over the top of them again. 'Where's Murray?'

'Packing his bags, rolling his swag,' said Michelle.

'How long is he going for?' asked Father Lemon.

'He'll be back late February in time for ag college,' said Michelle.

Fairly soon they were settled around the kitchen table and Millvan was slogging beers back along with the rest of them. A storm had approached and was rumbling in the distance. It was close. Millvan was edgy and sore.

'Elijah was a man with country like ours,' Father Lemon was saying, 'and he prayed earnestly that it would *not* rain, and it did not rain on the earth for three years and six months. Haggai did it too, both good men of God. So you see, God seems to like it dry. That's why he likes us Australians.'

'Yeah but they were good men you say? Hell, I'd kill any bastard wishing us all a drought.' A huge clap of thunder shook the house.

'Noah was good, the rest who were bad got drowned. If you're good you stay dry!' said the priest. 'I wish I could stay dry but that is where the Lord is ambiguous: drink heartily, he said, for the benefits of grain shall not be wasted.'

'You do a good sermon,' said Flynn, taking the mickey.

'Let us drink to you,' he replied.

Father Lemon smoked like a bushfire. He always had one half burned and hanging from his lip. As he reached into his pocket for another cigarette he accidentally pushed out a ten-dollar note. It dropped to the floor and Donny leant down to pick it up. He held it up to find the watermarks then absent-mindedly creased it into a tiny square.

Lemon went on: 'Millvan, you should come to mass more often if you want it to rain.'

Millvan stooped a little humbly. 'But how would you have us at mass when there's so much work to be done?'

Father Lemon gave his apologetic face.

'The trees and winds don't stop living come Sunday and neither should I.'

'I suppose you're right,' said the priest, 'but you'll burn yourself out that way.'

'Who's Mary Gilmore?' interrupted Donny. Then he read from the ten dollar note. 'No foe shall steal our harvest or sit on our stockyard rail.'

Suddenly Michelle yelled across the room: 'Can you hear that thunder?'

'That should be a law,' said Millvan to Donny. 'I've got a fat bastard bending my best rail.'

Michelle yelled again. 'If you don't try your rain dance now it'll be too late.'

They laughed along with her but didn't move.

'It must have been a law once,' continued Millvan.

'But it ain't any more,' said Donny. 'Those days of equity must have died with Mary.'

'Mighty craic—whoever thought to write that on our money?'

'The Treasury probably,' said Father Lemon. 'Anyone getting money for nothing wants to make the means noble-sounding.'

'Nothing noble about those arses,' said Millvan.

'Right time for a rain dance,' said Flynn, warming up. 'There's thunder out yonder,' he said in his best yokel accent.

'It's gone quiet all of a sudden,' said Michelle.

'Well all the more reason for it,' yelled Donny. He swigged hard at his bottle. Then he shuffled into the centre of the room and, to Terry's amazement, he began to bend his knees and move to an inaudible rhythm.

Michelle began to laugh.

'You imbecile,' she muttered.

'The key is having a good time,' said Donny. He looked like an Indian dancing around a fire in a Western.

'I think that makes fifty points already,' said Millvan after they'd stopped laughing.

Just then a boom of thunder cracked overhead. Terry's jaw dropped open in disbelief as some spots of rain hit the roof.

'It'll rain,' said Flynn.

But the storm swung by to the north, exactly as it had done earlier. They got the edge of it and despite another rain dance it dropped only enough to slick the gutters and crust the dust. Millvan knew that the tail of the system was gone. It was too late for a summer crop. He'd need the pine now and have to work even harder than before.

After Murray came out with his gear Flynn said it was time to go. He wanted to leave for town early in the morning.

'Fuck the rain, eh,' said Millvan as they filed out. 'Who needs it anyway?'

They saw through his bravado straightaway.

'I'll do another rain dance tomorrow,' joked Donny. 'On the law of averages it's got to work sooner or later.'

Michelle laughed.

'Come to mass,' said Father Lemon.

Flynn told Millvan he would help him with the rest of the pine. He said he would be down shortly. Donny nodded. He would help also.

Michelle gave Murray a big hug as he left. Millvan shook Murray's hand, slapped him on the shoulder and told him to learn as much as he could and not to drink too much. 'And try to stay on your horse,' he yelled as Murray and Flynn got into the ute.

The tail has gone through now, remembered Millvan the next morning, *and it is too late for a summer crop.*

So I'll have to work harder.

From then on he worked and only rested to eat and sleep. When it got hot he kept hauling logs and when he needed a drink he didn't take it, not even during the middle of the afternoon when the wind dropped dead.

When he finally came home each night he took to sleeping in the verandah chairs. Falling asleep with the calm of the night and the stars like dinner plates to remind him of the stock route and when he was the boy.

Michelle would put a blanket on him when she came to get his dishes. In the morning he was gone before the birds and he did not truly speak to his wife for two weeks.

That was what made her worried till she begged the others to come and help him just as she had begged them to come and see him after harvest. Flynn arranged for the Larkham brothers to work his place whilst he helped out and Donny got away from his place too. So they came willingly but he would start before them in the mornings and finish much later than they did, almost begrudgingly at the end of the day.

'He must still be a bit sore in the mouth,' said Flynn to Donny one afternoon.

'He doesn't speak to me much either.'

'We ought to cheer him up.'

'Shhh here he comes.'

'Let's go fishing when this is all over,' yelled Donny loudly as they chained down the logs onto the truck.

'Let's go next weekend,' said Flynn.

'We'll all take bobbing poles,' said Donny. 'I'll organise the bait.'

'We could go chasing cod up the river a bit,' said Flynn.

'Near Worten's?'

'Yeah, up that way a bit.'

'Or we could go to the lake,' said Donny. 'It's nice and calm and I could read in between bites.'

'The lake's good for perch too,' said Flynn.

Millvan stopped and turned slowly to look at them. The others watched him.

'We could go to the lake,' he said slowly. He straightened his back. Flynn and Donny watched him wipe his sweaty forehead then place his hands on the small of his back and stretch again.

'Sure we could and we will,' said Flynn.

'We will,' said Millvan, 'but when this is all over. I've still got so much work to do, I tell you,' he said.

'But out here,' began Flynn, 'life should always be treated like a lake.'

'What do you mean?'

'Well, despite a lake being used for something different altogether, it should *also* be used for recreational purposes.'

'We could go fishing next weekend,' said Donny.

'I can't, mate. Hell, I'd kill to go fishing next weekend but there's a lot of pine to be cut yet.'

'We could,' said Flynn.

'Nah, afterwards when it's all done. It feels better when everything is done.'

That afternoon Donny and Flynn slipped off early to tidy a few things up but Millvan stayed on working late into the long evening.

When Millvan finally came home dirty and scabbed he saw that Donny and Flynn were drinking beer at a card table on the back verandah. They must have brought the beer themselves, he thought. He felt like a beer and was glad for it. He walked over to them smiling. 'Tidied things up I suppose?'

The pair of them just smiled back and kept sipping on their beer and nothing was said. He took a beer, thanked them for it and then sat with them in the quiet. It was pleasant that no one spoke.

There was a water pump running and a radio on in the background. Dragonflies flew in the garden and some little black mosquitoes bit the men's arms. The sun dipped out behind the trees and all the reds flared and paled to a light blue and then it was night. Night was a bold dark blue sky growing bolder. The pump died and the radio became clear in the air. It was a big bass line jumping through the ground. If you were up close there would be more to hear but only the bass came through the ground. Someone must have left the radio on in the ute. It wasn't turned up loud. Only loud enough to hear if you were driving and it was parked over a hundred metres away. The air sure was clear.

Millvan just sat and sipped and the other pair smiled at each other from time to time and sipped at their beer too.

They watched the stars come out and with them came the bugs. There were crickets making a constant scratching and another sort of insect doing a slower click. Someone had turned on the dim verandah light. Millvan didn't notice, he was too tired. Bugs and big wood moths butted into the halo of the light and into the luminous white of everyone's foreheads and arms and walked down their shirts. Millvan got up and walked out into the clearing to piss. The air was cool and it was so quiet he felt happy for the first time in days.

When he came back the other two were smiling about something. Then, far away, a rumble sounded the dogs off and they all ran out into the driveway, barking and running into each other. Some big beams broke over the ridge and waved about the night sky looking for the downward slope, then found it as a car appeared on the ridge. Millvan stirred a little in his chair. 'Who's this?'

'How the bloody hell should we know,' leered Flynn loudly, 'it's your place. We're just trying to have a quiet beer.' Meanwhile the car had driven slowly to the front of the house and stopped but Millvan couldn't see who it was with only the dim car light on. He heard opening doors and laughing people. Then he heard Father Lemon's rasping voice. Then the dogs started again, more lights on the ridge. He looked at the other two sitting there with wide and toothy grins. 'Suppose you two organised a fucking party?'

They laughed at him then and he clapped them both on the back. 'Feel like a beer then or what?' he asked them.

A few hours later nine more cars had unloaded people and a row of drinking men had formed along the verandah. Inside a gaggle of women were talking in circles and occasionally passed things out to the men who were cooking the barbecue. Kids ran past them playing funny buggers and every so often the little ones cried out about the burrs.

Even later on they all ate together and there was a line up to the barbecue. Everyone talked and by and by the music became louder.

Then the little ones fell asleep.

Amongst the adults, familiar circles had formed. There was still one outside on the verandah, one in the living room. Millvan, Flynn, Donny, Father Lemon and Ross Healy were in the kitchen. Ross was a friend from way over the other side of the district and Millvan hadn't seen him regularly since they'd gone to the rodeos together. Millvan was glad to have him there. He'd packed on a huge beer gut since Millvan had seen him last.

Terry wandered in from outside and joined them. He'd been in the stables drinking the two bottles of beer he'd stolen earlier in the night. He still wasn't that good with alcohol and he could feel it inside his skull. Nevertheless, he wanted more. When the right moment came he would ask his father if he could have another beer. He could never tell when his father was drunk. Unlike Donny, he thought.

Donny was the drunkest of them all and was dancing in the corridor.

'He knows how to dance all right,' said Flynn to everybody.

Donny winked and clicked, his head went from left to right.

'Probably learnt it in Vietnam,' said Terry daringly. He'd spoken before he could stop himself. It had just come out.

Donny came in from the corridor and sat down.

Nobody said anything.

Everyone looked down but Terry looked around with wide eyes. He wanted to see what would happen. Outside they heard laughing but no one at the table said a word.

And as Millvan had expected, the dancing went all out of Donny. He looked very old and sat slumped in his chair.

Millvan told Terry to go away.

'But what did I do?' he asked innocently.

'Go to bed.'

'No,' said Donny softly, 'it's nothing.'

He paused for a long time then opened his throat to a whole beer.

'We learnt . . . to dance all right. Everybody did over there. If you weren't sitting in having a smoke then you were out dancing.'

Millvan lowered his eyes. He'd heard this story before, so had Flynn. *Bloody kid*, he thought.

'There were some good bars in Saigon, too, where gooks weren't allowed. They didn't like dancing anyway. Not in a bar, not in a party. You never saw them doing it.

'So one time our platoon made some hostage Vietcong dance along the road to keep the soldiers entertained. We were taking them back to base. Two guys kept the little fuckers going like that for hours. It was funny at the time because we hated the treacherous little bastards.' Donny shook his head and breathed deeply.

'These two guys in my platoon, one was an American, the other was an Aussie I think . . . they thought it was really funny. They might have been high. They made them do dances and went through the process of demonstrating how they wanted them to dance. They laughed like crazy when they did the hula-hula. Do it again, they'd say, pissing themselves laughing. Do it again! After about ten times the Vietcong showed their discontent. Before then they'd been too scared. That's when these two idiots got mean and kept them going. They pushed them on for miles and wouldn't even let them stop to pee. Finally, when the little fuckers couldn't hold on any more, they danced off the side of the road with their dicks out to piss. That's when the soldiers shot them. Those two were just waiting for an excuse to justify the killing. Going off the road constituted an escape attempt. But the shots made one of the other gooks shit his pants in fear and then he was shot for stinking, dancing with shit in his pants, boom, and bloody dead.

'They made them dance,' he went on slowly. 'They made them do that for over twenty miles down the road with us on the way to the next base. They said do a jig, do a jig!'

Donny stopped and shook his head. Millvan watched him silently. Flynn was looking at him sternly and hadn't taken a drink from his bottle.

'I remember the whole platoon laughing too. Little fuckers,' he spat. 'Then we got a radio call saying they didn't need them at the base any more.' Donny spoke quickly now. 'We laughed at them and then we shot them. We were ordered to,' he said coldly. 'I don't let it bother me any more. I don't let it bother me because it wasn't my idea and I can't be bothered thinking about it anymore.' He folded his arms and hunched into his chair.

'Shit,' said Terry, loud in the silence.

'Nothing bothers me anymore,' he said. Then he finished his new bottle of beer with a long swig. He got up and stumbled back outside.

Terry turned to Millvan after Donny left.

'I don't want to talk about it,' said Millvan firmly.

Father Lemon made the sign of the cross and muttered under his breath.

Donny burped loudly from down the hall.

'That wasn't good,' said Flynn. 'Terry, can you fetch me a bottle out of the cabinet?'

He nodded sadly.

'Get the Bundy.'

He came back with the bottle and a glass for himself.

'Can I, Dad?'

'Just one.'

'I'll make it a good one then,' said Flynn. He winked at Millvan. 'Those fellas who went over there, I heard of a bloke who came back and thought the ceiling fans was choppers. Poor bastard would go RAHHHHH whenever it got hot and you had to turn the bloody fans on.'

They all shook their heads. Father Lemon made the sign on his chest again. Then they saw Donny coming back and they all dreaded it but they saw he had regained his composure and so they put it behind them and forgot it. Like they forgot the droughts and didn't think of them in a good season.

Later on, when the eldest kids had fallen asleep and the music had been switched right down, the women began to help Michelle clean the kitchen and the men were discussing whether Millvan should double crop wheat to deal with his debt.

Ross Healy was saying: 'You ought to always treat the soil like a fragile glass . . .' The others nodded their heads wisely.

'. . . but this time you have to treat it like the rum in the glass.'

'It's the rum in the glass that Rawlings wants,' said Millvan.

'Too right, the pig.'

'Well you don't have to make a deal with the bastard,' said Donny all of a sudden. He sat up and his languid eyes widened a little. 'I think you ought to compromise.'

'Well how do you do that?' said Flynn. 'You're so cut you wouldn't know a good idea from a sack of dags. The other day you said, "I've got a good idea," so we put the foot valve in the silt hole and sucked the pump full of mud. Good thinkin' that was.'

'The bloody main dam was out of water,' he said quickly, but he didn't let himself get drawn in.

'You don't have to make a deal, you know,' Donny continued.

'So how then?' asked Millvan.

'Well I thought of it the other day as I was chopping wood left behind by those arsehole loggers.'

'Don't go asking me whether I'm insured,' Millvan butted in.

'This is no scam!' Donny cried. 'And it could get you rich. All day I was thinking about it and looking at the country and I decided, why cut out a little timber and then blow an O-ring for the next five years? Why not burn all the timber out and put it under wheat and next year when he calls you in after harvest you can say, I'm through with your busted deals. And those loggers can go get fucked.'

'Nah, I'll be right with just the pine.'

'What about this talk of needing more wheat?'

Millvan sighed and shifted and shook his head. 'Yeah, I thought about cutting all the trees down too but I don't think I could take it out. That timber's been left there and Grandpa and Dad left it thick and I don't think I should do things different on account of my bad times. They had plenty of bad times and left it there.'

'But it could get you rich!'

'I dunno about that.'

'Bugger me!' said Donny. 'I don't see why we don't all help put through a big fire and then plant wheat. It'd be time well spent.'

'You don't have to help me if you don't want to. I always said that,' said Millvan.

Donny calmed and said he was sorry. 'I didn't mean that. We all want to help you but we might as well make a good go of it.'

'How would you do it?' asked Millvan. 'There's five years of work between us getting that ready without dozers and scrub chains.'

'Yeah, how does your good idea factor that?' asked Flynn.

Donny turned on a grilled cheese with the lot smile.

'We'd burn,' he said excitedly over his empty glass. 'Let a huge fire go through next month when it all dries off and gets hot so you sink.'

'Numbers fifteen or one of those verses,' began Father Lemon, grinning drunkenly. 'Fire is a soothing aroma to the Lord.' He was trying hard to put on a serious face, 'Burn it for the Lord and give thanks!'

Millvan smiled. It was mad and out of hand. He saw Grandpa's trees and Donny's crazed gleam and with regret he realised he was thinking about burning it all and growing more wheat.

'Then we'll send in the axes,' continued Donny, 'and the rakes and then the deep ripper and the rakes again. It's good earth, rich. That's what it's there for and with a good burn we can have three-quarters of the job done before you know it.'

'I dunno,' said Millvan and Donny shook his head with frustration.

'You're too bloody superstitious. If you don't look at this properly you'll wind up with nothing. You go on and on with your way of things but what if it doesn't rain all summer? Then you're screwed, that's what,' he said madly.

Millvan listened, thought of burning it, putting it all under wheat, and came back to Donny tailing off with, 'If you don't bloody burn, all the helping hands we can give you will come to nothing.'

Flynn looked down at his boots and Millvan, in that second, understood that they couldn't help him forever. They were telling him in the nicest possible way that if he didn't burn the river timber he'd end up with nothing. Arbour would be auctioned off and he'd have plenty of time to think about whether his forefathers would have endorsed the fact he hadn't burnt.

Donny continued. 'You've got to cut out this bloody superstitious looking-after-Grandpa's-trees shit.'

'He's maybe right there,' said Flynn. 'You're gunnna be in the shit if it doesn't rain.'

Millvan nodded and looked at the ground. 'I have got a rake ready to go.'

'So have I,' said Donny, 'and he's got a ripper he'll lend to you.' He pointed at Flynn. Flynn nodded

'It's thick with organics and think of the subsoil moisture!'

'I suppose we wouldn't even need a rain to plant on,' said Millvan.

'Ah sweet virgin soil!' said Donny. 'How many acres you think are in there?'

'Probably a few thousand,' said Millvan. 'There's a lot of country in that big stripe all the way along the river, west of the house there.'

'It'll get you rich,' said Donny, 'and we won't have to chop any more bloody stumps. I've had it up to my ears with them.'

'It's a good thing it didn't rain the other day then,' said Millvan.

Donny nodded excitedly; 'We don't want any rain at all. It's better! How can we burn when it's wet?'

'I never wanted to take it though,' said Millvan. 'Grandpa and Dad left it there but I suppose they had better soils back then. And Murray needs something fresh to start with.' He felt excited. It'd be for him that we'd do it. Yes,' he said. 'We'll take the lot and put it back to beautiful rows of cultivation for Murray. He needs some new country. I can see it now. This place is drained like me.'

'Ha ha,' said Donny, turning to Flynn and poking him in the belly. 'You see!'

'Well you can laugh now but you won't laugh getting mud out of that pump tomorrow, and it won't get you rich.'

'But at seven or eight bags an acre and with the money from the timber it'd kill off Rawlings's little stake,' said Millvan. 'It could even bugger his hands off completely and then I could give it to Murray. He needs something fresh, like when we got it given to us.'

'That's right,' said Donny.

'I'd help you put a burn through if you needed me,' said Ross Healy.

'Me too,' said Father Lemon.

Millvan thanked them and his eyes began to glaze with the thoughts of the new earth. He saw the shadows in the rows and could smell the newly lifted earth in his hands, taste the dust in the back of his throat, and he saw Murray sitting in the tractor looking backwards out of the cab down at the new tyre marks roll out and get chopped under the planter.

'The worst thing is,' said Millvan suddenly, 'we'll have to get those loggers back in. If I am going to burn I'd want the good timber out of there and I can't do that and get it ready to burn by myself.'

'That won't be so hard,' said Donny.

'Yeah,' said Flynn flexing his muscles. 'I could get that pimp Roggerson to whore any time I wanted.'

'You're liable to do a hip in, you old bastard,' said Ross Healy to Donny.

'Nah, it's just a situation of forceful negotiation. Give them something they want and tell them something like, I'll stay a mile either side of your hunting paddock of choice. That way they'll be sure they won't even see you.'

'I don't want to let the bastards shoot.'

'You said it yourself they won't come back.'

'Maybe then, maybe,' said Millvan, throwing up his arms. 'Enough of all that for one night.'

So they went back to their party and didn't leave it till early the next morning.

He woke up before the others and took his coffee out on to the steps as usual.

'Rouger my old boy, where the bloody hell have you been?'

The dog was sunning himself on the other side of the peppercorn.

'Come here, boy. Come on.'

Rouger ambled over stiff-legged at first and then relaxed and wagged his tail. Millvan patted the dog's nose and grated behind his ears. 'Where the hell have you been?'

The dog stared up into Millvan's face and let himself be caressed behind the ears.

'Come on, boy, we'll go for a walk.'

He placed his unfinished coffee on the steps and walked out past the shed to the edge of the clearing. The dog ran ahead of him happily and smelt at the grasses as if he was hunting. They went over the fence at the edge of the clearing and out through the trees towards the river.

'Did you run off this way?' he asked him. 'If this is

where you go you'd better savour it, boy, because by May it'll be under cultivation.' His head stung a little from the night before but he hadn't forgotten the excitement of the idea that Murray would get new dirt.

Soon he was in amongst the trees of the river block.

Get a stack of wheat and another stack of wheat—easy, thought Millvan. That's what Arbour needs.

He thought slowly through his hangover.

Why did men care about what their grandfathers had left behind? That was being sentimental. Being sentimental was not the way of things. 'The way of things is the law of nature,' he said aloud. 'The law of nature says, may the best man win, hey boy? To you they say, run away and hunt.'

Where did that dog go? He stopped and whistled. 'COME HERE.' Nothing happened. He whistled again. Finally he saw the dog ramble back over a distant part of the river-bank. He still had its nose down to the ground. 'You're a bugger of a thing sometimes,' Millvan said gently. The dog looked up at him once then ambled off on a sheep pad, nose down, ears pricked.

Millvan let him go.

He walked quietly for some time and counted quite a number of small pine clumps still standing. If he was ever going to burn then he'd have to get the loggers back in to cut this. He couldn't burn it. He looked around at the calm trees that had never known an axe. He could hear the cockatoos and plenty of other morning birds. It'd burn all right, no doubt about it.

It'd make way for winter wheat. He tore a switch off a nearby wattle tree. Yellow flowers meant spring was still here. Summer's real heat was yet to come. He walked on past bloodwood and belah and waved the switch at butterflies tending to pollen in the grasses. He walked through a clump of towering bloodwood. He'd always enjoyed walking through these old trees. But they'd grow back. He suddenly felt something in his chest that ached. *You are probably lonely*, he told himself, but when he whistled for the dog and he came, the feeling didn't go away. *They'll grow back*, Millvan repeated.

Then aloud he cursed the sky. 'If I could just plant a summer crop,' he said angrily.

'Why couldn't you just up and rain?' He rubbed at his sore jaw, spotted a bright lorikeet eating the honey pollen of a bottlebrush and cursed again.

But the way of things is how to make a buck. Any bloke would do the same and I am just too sentimental. But if the law of nature says I should burn then I will.

He finished counting the pine clumps, turned around and walked home.

He rang the number. It was Roggerson. He didn't want to send his boys back.

'That's all right,' said Millvan. 'You tell them it wasn't anything.'

'They won't come back.'

'They'll get paid. They know where to go and what to do. You tell them they won't even have to see me. You tell them I'll give them something extra as well.'

The static hissed up the wire. Roggerson didn't say anything.

'You tell them they can shoot whatever hops out of my fire. We're lighting up a big patch of timber full of kangaroos and pigs. They can take whatever they kill. They can have those skins and pigs for free.'

'What if you pay them a little extra as well?'

'Nah, they can have what hops out. Plus what they cut and cart. That's a fair bit already and the extra can be what they kill.'

Roggerson said he'd tell them about it.

'Tell them quick. I need to know tonight or tomorrow morning.'

Roggerson rang back half an hour later.

'They'll come back but only if you set up the ambush so they get everything.'

'They'll get what they don't miss,' said Millvan.

They came three days later and set up camp at the same gully on the river. During the following weeks they cut the rest of the pine and carted it to the mill and Millvan received his first cheque.

Finally he felt as if he had things ready and agreed to go fishing with Donny and Flynn in the lake.

'The pine did well,' said Millvan to Donny as they fished. They had been at the lake all morning and had already caught three nice perch on the bob.

'Cheers to those fires on the coast last year then,' said Terry.

'You should never cheer another's misfortune, young man,' said Donny.

'Whatever,' shrugged Terry.

'If you do, misfortune will rain just over your boundary fence, frost your flats and give your dog blue balls so he greets the bank man with a smile on his face.'

Flynn chuckled and Millvan smiled. Donny and Terry had spoken a lot since the night of the party.

'Those poor bastards growing pine had the equivalent of thirty years of wheat crops burnt to the ground,' continued Donny. 'All the bloody eucalyptus and wattle grew back then and they had to cut it out. You and your old man should think yourselves lucky in comparison.'

'Why didn't they replant pine instead of eucalyptus?' asked Terry.

'They didn't plant the shit. Don't you know after a fire anything native grows back? Australian plants are all adapted to it; banksia wouldn't survive without bushfires . . . its seeds don't split till they're baked right through. See that old gum over there?' Beside the point where they fished was a particularly tall tree.

'It's probably seen a dozen fires.'

'Well how is burning going to get ground ready if they like fire?'

'A fire will kill most of it,' said Millvan.

'Yeah, but you still have to chop at it afterwards. It won't do all the work for you and if you don't till the soil straightaway all the germinated seeds spring up,' said Donny.

'It's funny how a fire will germinate seeds,' said Millvan.

'Getting it ready to plant isn't going to be funny,' said Flynn.

'We've got work to do.'

'A lot.'

'Hang on, I'm getting a bite,' said Donny.

The others immediately turned to watch his line for a few seconds then looked anxiously at their own.

'It's sucking on it like a carp.'

'You can never tell what it is from the bite,' scoffed Millvan.

'I bet it's a carp,' whispered Donny.

Almost at once he jerked the line upwards and it sprang to life in his hand. It bounced and went from left to right then deep and suddenly flapped as it came to the surface and showed its tail to the men.

'You lucky bastard.'

'What is it?'

'I don't know but it's no guppy.'

'It's a big carp!' yelled Millvan. 'I saw from it's tail.'

'No, it's another perch.'

It was a nice perch. Donny hauled the fish up onto the bank, took the hook out of its mouth and then put it with the others in the sugar sack.

'Not a bad fish,' said Millvan.

'Enjoy your little moment while it lasts,' said Flynn to Donny.

Donny smiled at them.

Over the following months they prepared for the burn. Mostly Millvan and Terry made firebreaks. They graded roads all around and into the river block so the pine could be taken out, every last log. Millvan concentrated on the firebreaks to the east so that the big westerly would eventually push the fire onto them and burn itself out in the dust. The westerly blew all summer long. The cricket tests ran into the one-dayers and players came and went like the summer storms; some hit but most missed. The ground cracked open and the grass crunched to dry powder underfoot.

Most of the work was getting rid of the timber. Sometimes the others helped him but mostly it was his sweat that got it done.

The Christmas period came and went then drifted quickly into January when the drying sun was always heavy. When the loggers finished in mid January Millvan knew it was time.

On the day they were to burn, Millvan awoke to have breakfast with Michelle when it was still dark. Then dawn squeezed through and it was morning. The birds were singing strong and it was pleasant but you could tell it was going to be very hot. It was already hot in the first touch of sun. Millvan greased and oiled the bikes and truck and by the time he had finished dragging out hessian bags and filling water tanks it was already eight o'clock. The men started to arrive as he walked back to the house. The westerly was dry and faint and he was sweating. It was very hot. He made coffee for them as they talked; they drank it on the verandah and by the time they'd finished they were all sweating.

'That's a desert wind that one,' said Keithy, 'straight off the dunes. The real summer's come a week early.' The others nodded.

Drinking coffee with Millvan were Donny, Flynn, Ross Healy and Keithy. Terry was hanging around impatiently. Millvan had insisted he stay home with Michelle to help the men when they came back to reload the water tanks. There was another cloud of dust and a couple more utes arrived. Dave and Will Larkham had brought a ute full of hessian bags. The dingo dog came over till he was a small distance away and sat smiling at them.

'Come here,' ordered Millvan.

The dog came further, head down, till he was in front of Millvan's knees. He petted him and the dog nuzzled. Then he ruffled his ears. 'Don't you bloody run away today,' he told the dog.

Keithy was talking about how he'd seen the Roggersons at the pub. 'They weren't too happy about coming back here.'

'What did they say?'

'Or just stuff like, "If he even looks sideways at me I'll smash him," and stuff like that.'

'I'll bloody smash him,' said Donny.

'They'd be worried to hear you say that,' said Flynn.

The dog started smiling again and was still smiling, thumping dust with his tail, as the men wandered over to greet Father Lemon by the shed.

Dave and Keithy started smoking together by the old T-Ford tractor. It had a blade on it for pushing breaks and piling up timber. Michelle brought over some coffee and a big jug of iced cordial to keep them happy in waiting.

Will Larkham was wearing his white five-gallon hat and was sitting with his legs hanging out of his brother's truck. Alongside were some wheat bags, a chainsaw, two axes and a spray unit hanging out of a couple of forty-four gallon drums.

The sky was blue and very high. It seemed there was no atmosphere at all.

Donny was humming out a song: you could hear it in between the lulls in the wind and the noise of what he was doing. Lugging petrol cans and spilling the mixture into the fire burners and stopping from time to time to whistle it instead.

'Give it a bloody rest eh,' said Keithy.

Finally when the fire-starter cans were full, the pumps primed and the sun heavy, they got ready to drive out. Two motorbikes, a tractor with a blade and the loaded truck set off from the shed.

The two Larkham brothers drove the motorbikes and Michelle waved them off. Ross Healy followed in the tractor. Millvan's truck pulled out slowly and men scrambled to climb aboard.

'Jump on her—she likes to be jumped,' yelled Keithy from the back of the truck. 'The old girl's been around.' Father Lemon clambered over the side with his gut hanging out of his button-up shirt.

'At least she came with a manual. My missus—crikey! I need a manual.'

Now Keithy was on about how he got in trouble with his wife when he got home from the pub.

'All women should come with a manual.'

Michelle ignored him and he winked at her.

'. . . Give them an overhaul every five years.' She feigned throwing something at him and he laughed delightedly. 'Just joshing.'

The old truck rumbled out to the river block. Millvan drove along freshly graded tracks. Those on the back couldn't hear the cricket on the radio so they watched the countryside. It took half an hour of jolting past clumps of tall gums, down and up a dry channel full of trampled reeds, over a sand ridge where the arse end of the truck slipped out and cornered close to the fence, and finally past a quiet flat where three old trees towered high as eagles. A big buck roo jumped out onto the road in front of the truck and went through the fence so fast it tripped on the wires and cartwheeled into a tree. Out of the front came a 'Hee, hee, hee'. The bush was monotonous and still as if it knew what it was in for. Eventually they came through the light suckers and low bush that ran down to the heavy timber of the river block. They drove past the red loggers' truck on the edge of it. One of them waved but the others just sat in the dirt and didn't look up. Ross Healy saw one of them sharpening a knife as he drove past later on the tractor. The river block stretched out far and there were no hills and you could only see a hundred metres or so into the tangle. They ran over a big red-bellied black just before they got to the end of the block.

'Bastard!' said somebody in the cabin. 'Check it comes out the back.' It was twisting and biting the bloody patches, and probably already half dead.

'Did it come out the back?'

Flynn banged on the cabin roof to answer.

He could hear Donny explain: 'The bastards get flicked up and caught under the chassis then drop down and bite you when you stop.'

'He came out the back all right.'

The river was shaped like the snake. It made s-shaped loops and turns all the way from the house through the ridges.

It was to be a hell of a big fire, big and hot. The westerly was steady in their faces as they waited for the brothers to appear through the truck's dusty wake. By the time Ross Healy finally arrived in his tractor it was approaching high noon.

'Right, let's do her,' said Millvan. 'I want to get back before the tea break to check on the cricket.'

Donny dropped the first match. Dave and Will set off on the motorbikes as he did so. Woof!—the fuel caught and a big clump of cane grass went up in bright red flames. It crackled loudly and puffed green smoke.

'That'll do the trick. Maybe we'll flush out a pig.'

'There'll be a few holed up in there somewhere,' said Millvan smiling. 'Those bastard Roggersons will have all the fun though.'

Over to the north side of the timber they'd lit up as well. The two-stroke bikes drowned out the crackling of their fires but they could see flames beginning to take.

Keithy called out with his fire burner. 'Go?'

'Yep, push off,' yelled Millvan. He lit the wick and walked off dripping flames out of the burner down the dirt track. Before long they couldn't see him any more. But through the trees they could see his fire start as a little red line that drew off towards the east. The big westerly pushed it nicely. Millvan and Donny watched the first tree start to take. It was a little wilga that grew out of a dried-out channel full of tall cane grass. The fire had raced into the grass with enough wind behind it to combust the green leaves. Then the branches were burning and it made them happy to see how much heat there was.

'Couldn't get a better day for it,' said Donny.

'Yep,' said Millvan happily. 'By May this'll all be cultivation and Murray will grow high-protein wheat.'

'Virgin soil will give it to you.'

'It's just a pity he's away. He would learn being here. If he were here I'd have him with me the whole time.'

Donny nodded but the fire was getting too loud to hear the talk. Then he exploded with excitement. 'Look at her go!' he yelled.

The trees and the big wind had begun to twist and buckle in the heat. The red cinders showed the wind beginning to spin around the trees like a whirly-wind spinning dust in the desert. 'That's what you call the wall!' yelled Donny. 'That's what we want!'

'Let's go,' shouted Millvan. 'I can't hear a thing.' They went to the truck and climbed in. Millvan got in the driver's side.

'Look at her go,' said Donny. 'That's a wall all right. That's the hottest you can get it. Not even the wind affects it. See how it makes its own system.'

Smoke billowed out onto the road. They could feel the heat. The wind had created a draw from all directions that sucked in the air and made the wind whistle. The fire was even in the air between the trees. It raced with the hot currents and roared. Cinders exploded everywhere and buffeted towards the east like sails in a red armada.

'The wind is still pushing it,' said Millvan. 'There must be less resistance on the other side.'

'I heard a story once,' yelled Donny excitedly, 'about a big draw on a patch of scrub that burnt in and made a system and despite the wind it made clouds of moisture above it and it actually rained.' Millvan was grinning. 'It's not that big yet but we should drive around to the north and check the firebreaks again.'

'Yeah but we don't have to worry,' said Donny. 'With that wind it's like you said—it'll burn out against the breaks.'

'Nothing else to do,' said Millvan complacently, starting the truck. 'We can listen to the cricket.'

It took around twenty minutes to get to the breaks they'd pushed up. They cut through the bush on either side of the track. It looked a long way for a fire to jump. Ross Healy was there grading some new breaks with the little T-Ford.

He'd pushed the top inch of soil and grass off to make strips through the bluegrass paddocks. It was an old track he'd started with and now it was as wide as a tennis court. In some places it was shiny where the blade had cut the clays clean and pressed them.

Healy raised the blade, moved the tractor around and turned it off. He walked over to them. 'That'll do,' Millvan yelled to him from out of the cab. 'Come on.'

'How's it burning back there?'

'Like jungle fever.'

'Hell, it's hot enough,' said Healy, 'Melt a fuckin' cactus.' He jumped up onto the truck tray and slapped the roof of the cab to indicate he was ready.

As Millvan was reversing the truck around they saw a motorbike speeding towards them. They got out of the truck. It was Will Larkham. He came up sweating and dusty, looking dead worried, and spoke quickly to them for over a minute. Millvan and Donny stood beside him and paled as he spoke. Occasionally they looked behind him, looked off into the distance from where he'd come from and up at the leaves of the trees.

'How far?' asked Millvan finally. He kicked at the ground to bring up dust.

'A full one hundred and eighty degrees!' Then the many expletives men save for such times.

'She's got away. Look at that wind,' he pointed to the dust he'd made.

It had turned into an easterly.

'It's swung a mile on us.'

Will cringed. 'Flynn nearly got stuck and Dave had to come and get him on the bike. We put out water but it didn't do anything.'

'Fuck!'

Donny turned to Healy. 'Take the tractor and put in a break before the house.'

'Where's it gone?' asked Millvan. His face was like a bull's in the crush.

'Mostly to the north. It's burning through that grass paddock.'

'Hell, if it gets over into the neighbour's block, it'll burn for days. We can't let it get anywhere near that bugger's place. Take the truck and get the other men into the grass paddock.'

'Dave's already there.'

'Stop it in the paddock. Run over it in the truck if you have to. When you're finished, come back and get me off the firebreak in front of the house. Ross, don't go to the house yet. Follow me around the bend then head out to the grass paddock from the south. You can push up breaks as a reserve. Donny, you go with Will, I need as many blokes there as I can.'

'Righto, righto,' they said.

Donny got down out of the cab and onto the back of the motorbike and they drove off.

'Fuck, fuck, fuck,' yelled Millvan as he started the truck viciously and wrenched it into reverse. 'Fuck the wind.'

Healy said nothing.

Millvan waited till Healy had got the tractor to start then screamed the truck into gear and jerked it down the road. Healy swung the tractor into the truck's bull dust.

Millvan drove half blind. The smoke came in as thick pillows across the dirt track. Fleeing quails exploded past the cab. Flocks of cockatoos streaked by, squawking in panic. He saw the fire was already across the track. He could tell it was thin. He drove the truck straight through it. The heat flushed the cabin as he went through. Just after, the track split into two. The left led to the house. The right fork curved into thick scrub. He had changed his mind about going to the house break and didn't wait for Healy but turned into the thick scrub.

He cursed the wind and heat.

Now that the wind had changed, the fire was liable to run towards his cattle. He knew if the fire got close to them they'd panic and run through the fences. Then they'd have to be driven back in dribs and drabs from neighbours' musters. Some would be cut badly from the wire and have to be shot. Some would never come back, and you can't press neighbours for stock counts when they're already doing you a favour by bringing your cattle back. He couldn't afford to lose a single beast.

You'll fight it here before it gets to the cattle, he told himself.

He saw the direction the fire was pushing and calculated that if he held the fire back behind the track he could keep it away from the cattle. He and Terry had not pushed breaks where the cattle were. There was one thin fire he could see burning faster than the others but it wasn't yet over the old track. The flames there were not very tall. It seemed to be a grass fire. The old track was too thin to be a break but if he put out enough water he could certainly slow it down and maybe give the others time to come and help stop it before it broke through and got closer to the cattle.

You'll be able to hold it off here, he told himself. He had a truck with water and a pump to fight it with. The wind might turn around any minute.

Maybe the wind would change. Why couldn't it change back?

He raced the truck towards the grass fire. He stalled the old machine to stop it and climbed onto the tray. The pump fired with the first pull and soon the hose bucked against his grip. He wet the ground and logs ahead of the blaze. It rose up at him as it burnt through. With the wind behind it, the flames grew higher and higher till he had to raise the water up as a curtain over the truck and himself to block the heat. Soon his eyes were stinging with smoke.

After pumping out a lot of water he noticed that behind the smokescreen the fire seemed much smaller and thinner than before.

I can beat this, he thought. He reversed the whining old truck back to another section of fire burning further down the track. Once again he sprayed it then made the curtain and beat it down. He did this three more times in different places, each further down the way he'd come.

Bugger you, wind, he thought, *I can beat you.* But he knew the water was draining and the dread rose in him with the sound of the pump. Then he saw a glowing redness up ahead where he'd beaten down the first fire. Through the smoke he made out flames and even before he had jumped into the cabin and made it halfway back through the billowing smoke he knew the first fire he'd beaten had risen again and burnt over the track. *This may be what Donny called the wall,* he thought. Once again he drove the truck straight over the fire. There were higher flames this time.

He saw flames on either side of the truck and instead of continuing he reversed the truck out of them. For a short time flames clung to the tray and he heard a hissing ring come from under the bonnet. He heard a popping and a shrill metallic whistling. He stopped the truck and got onto the back again, burnt his hand on the metal then wet the whole truck down. The water was coming slower now but the hissing sound was gone. He got back into the cabin and drove away from the fire. He saw the whole block to the west was lit up. He saw towering flames flaring and leaping up into the smokescreen canvas of the horizon. The fire was being driven by a strong steady wind and it drove through the wood like a sharp nail.

There was just a little bit of water left now and he knew it was useless. He was puffing hard and coughing, it exhausted him.

'There's not enough air here!' he said aloud. He could taste the charcoal building in his throat and in the heat and smoke the situation began to get the better of him. He looked high into the red sky and saw grass parrots streaking through the whipping branches. They did not cry out as they had done when he ate breakfast that morning. He saw them confused with the fire.

He looked skywards once more and saw the smoke clouds sliding over. *Damn the wind to hell. Damn it blasted in hell.*

Before, he'd always thought of the wind as weather's messenger but now he knew it was his only hope.

He prayed for it to turn back.

Turn, you fuck. Go back. You don't have to bring me rain but help me keep my home. He was sure the others would help Michelle and Terry if the fire got close to the house.

He started to put out the last of the water. The wind had not changed and he cursed it.

Wind, you are going to kill me today. This place is big enough for both of us and you can go from it as you wish. Many days in summer the trees are still and it is hot and you are nowhere, yet you've sprung up now.

Now the water was gone and he realised it was useless to keep fighting from the truck.

He took a hessian sack and soaked it with the condensation that had gathered on the sides and lid of the water tank.

He left the truck where it was and no longer cared whether it burnt up or not. He took the wet sack and ran to the burning flank. It was much bigger to face up to than it had been from the back of the truck and it was scalding hot. But he met it anyway, and with one hand to shield his face and the other wielding the sack, he set to beating the fire out of the grasses. He brought the sack down each time from behind his head and once a live cinder flicked up and burnt his cheek but he kept pounding against the flank regardless.

Help me, wind, he prayed as he pounded. *Let's kill this thing.*

But the heat was so strong the fire couldn't stay out, only sprang back up. He continued whacking and swung harder but finally it got so hot the beard on his cheek singed and he saw that the wall was beginning to come through and he knew he had to run. He ran towards a window in the smoke. He ran till he could feel the fire on his neck no longer. As he ran he saw the sack had dried out. It was very black and had holes in it from the big embers and the molten logs he'd hit. *Maybe I should find the river and fight with it alongside me the whole way to the house.* He made it to the clearer air he'd seen.

The house should be all right, he worried as he ran. *It's too far from the timber to burn.*

He tried to remember if there was a woodpile by the back door or leaves clogging the gutters. Now he was glad Keithy had chopped out the big box tree by the window.

And peppercorns were not good firewood, he thought.

They were green and thick with that stinking sap. They shouldn't burn like this mongrel eucalyptus. *This mongrel country wants to burn.* The whole skyline was ablaze.

A man is not greater than a bushfire and the winds, he swore. *Bugger the wind.*

It was about this time that Healy found the others in the grass paddock and helped them stop the fire. Donny, Father Lemon, Keithy, Flynn and the Larkham boys had been doing as Millvan had done, skirmishing little fire fronts and winning little battles as they got continually pushed backwards. But when Healy arrived and began pushing up new breaks across the open plain, they won more and more little battles and quickly burned it out. In less than twenty minutes the fire was gone from the grass paddock. Then Donny asked after Millvan and why Healy had left him. Healy told him.

'Is he on the heavy timber side of the fire?' asked Father Lemon anxiously.

Healy shrugged his shoulders. 'I think he was going for the house.'

'I'll call Michelle and check,' said Keithy.

Keithy called Michelle on his radio and asked her, in such a way as to prevent her from worrying or suspecting the worst, if she'd seen Millvan. She hadn't. Suddenly they all scrambled towards the bikes and tractor. Flynn was quickest to start off and they had to chase hard to keep up with him.

He had taken one of the motorbikes. Dave, Father Lemon and Keithy climbed onto the back of Healy's tractor.

They dispersed when they arrived at the big river timber. Flynn and Will drove the bikes into the scrub and up and over the many logs lying on the ground. The rest of them shouted out to Millvan from the track.

I have to make it to the river, thought Millvan as he ran. *I need to wet this useless sack in any case.* He moved at a steady pace towards the river. Behind him the fire followed as an oscillating roar. He was out in front of where it was burning slowest, and from quick glances over his shoulder he found he was slowly pulling away from the fire. It was the wrong direction to be running to get to the house quickly, though, and he ran without stopping for a long time. It was tiring, like running in sand. Suddenly it occurred to him he was headed to where the loggers were.

How unlucky would it be to get shot right now. In that smoke he was just another shape to take a pot shot at.

There was just another few hundred metres to the ambush.

Still you'd have to be unlucky, he reminded himself. *Hell, there's a lot of smoke.* He was getting very close to where the loggers ought to be but he hadn't heard a single shot fired.

The bastards are probably waiting along their sights, he thought. *Nah, they would have driven off by now.*

He looked up ahead and slowed down to find the gully. There was no one in the top of the gully but they could have been further back in.

'HEY—OI!'

'OI—WHERE ARE YOU FUCKING DOGS?'

Deep down he knew they wouldn't be there but he couldn't help tingling. He'd hoped they'd been stupid enough to stay. Then they could have driven him home. But his calls remained unanswered.

'OI FUCKERS!' he yelled again. Just to make sure. *They didn't screw me as bad as this wind,* he thought. He wondered if it swung that bad all the time and he'd just never noticed it.

It'd never swung like that.

'Goddamn this smoke,' he swore under his breath.

BOOM! A big explosion sounded behind him.

Hell, that must have been the truck! Poor old girl.

It was a huge noise. It couldn't have been a gunshot but he had a little bit of doubt in his mind. Somewhere he remembered hearing you needed air for sound to travel. *Smoke takes the distance out. So maybe it was a shotgun. No, it was the bloody truck!* He continued running towards the river and didn't look back.

He was very close to the river when he saw his dog away through the trees. The dog was ahead of him and running from the fire. He hadn't seen Millvan yet. *I told the bastard*

of a thing to stay home, he thought angrily. He felt scared for the dog. The fire could easily trap the stupid thing and burn him alive. Then Millvan saw the bullock. It must have been taking a breather behind one of the dense little wilga trees.

It was the big rangy bullock that had bowled Murray over and been left in the river block. Millvan saw the dog race up and bark at it. The bullock was snorting. Every time the bullock turned and lowered its head as if to charge, the dog crouched back on his hind legs and barked. Sometimes the dog went from side to side on his front legs and ducked under a low wilga tree. But mostly the bullock trotted and the dog followed. The dog must have thought he was doing a very purposeful thing and the bullock was probably trying to find a clearing with no trees so it could line up the dog and barrel it.

He had to send the dog home.

Millvan tried to whistle as he was running but the whistle came out weak from his dry lips.

'COME HERE,' he yelled on the run. The dog kept going so he tried whistling again. Still he kept going but Millvan was sure the dog had heard him and that made him even angrier.

'COME HERE, YOU BASTARD!'

But the dog kept going and Millvan couldn't keep up with it. He lost sight of the dog as he went down the riverbank after the bullock. Millvan ran to where they'd disappeared.

He came over the riverbank and ran down to a half-submerged log to cup down handfuls of water. It was tepid in the boiling sun and muddy as carp but it was water. There was no smoke down in the riverbed but the dog and the bullock were nowhere to be seen.

When he got up from drinking river water he saw the fire was coming over the riverbank. It was moving even quicker than before. The trees he could see were alight and red. It was the hottest he had ever been and it scared him. Those flames stared him down quicker than any bullock. It buckled him. He didn't think to curse it and in the pain of it he could only lift his arms to shield his face and ears and fall away from it. He splashed water up onto his face and groaned to feel his cheek was blistered. Then he remembered it was from the ember that flicked up off the sack and it gave him a sort of resolve. He ran away from the closest flames. He wasn't burning yet and he knew he could hide from it underwater. *I could lie in the water till the worst of it went over. Get in deep and let it burn overhead. If man and water couldn't beat this thing together then nothing could.*

He looked around for the nearest deep-looking stretch. There was a good hole of water a little way up the river. He ran to it and waded into the brown water. He lost one of his boots in the mud. He looked up high through the smoke to see the sky. The sun was a tarnished silver ball behind the black air. He saw a wedge-tail eagle soaring high over the yanking trees. It circled above him. He knew they circled over fires to see what was flushed out. Smoke attracted them. He felt a twang of something jolt through him so he looked down and watched as the thin fires burnt up each bank.

He felt hunted.

He saw the smoke hanging high over the water and then he couldn't see the eagle any more. But he felt scared, like maybe it was watching him, and in his deepest voice he yelled for the other men.

'DONNY—FLYNN!' then 'FLYNN!' again. 'FLYNN!'

He felt hit from the shouting. It was useless. The fire was too loud. The branches roared and there was no air for the sound to travel. Just smoke. But the smoke didn't come down on the water like it hung on the ground. *Or did it?* If it dropped down onto the water he would asphyxiate. He studied the smoke to make sure it wasn't dropping down. After looking at it swirl about for a few moments he realised he couldn't tell and he stopped watching it lest he trick himself. *Men don't trick themselves*, he told himself. But he didn't want to slip away into a dream because of smoke inhalation. That was death without knowing it.

Millvan was scared as all hell then. Now he felt so scared the eagle may as well have sat on his shoulder and smiled at him. He felt like the water was all slippery and brown because the fire was on him and he couldn't stop thinking about how long it would take to burn over. When he lay down with his face half in half out of the water he looked into the trees and saw them all red above him.

If they burn out quick I'll hold tight and then get up and run upwind. Other blokes have done this plenty of times, he told himself reassuringly. Only you didn't hear of it much because they lived through it. You only heard about the ones who'd died doing it. Like the one who'd crawled into a horse trough during a grass fire and the one who'd jumped into his rainwater tank after trying to save his house. Those two died like crabs. Plenty of other blokes dove underwater and lived though a fire, he told himself. He purposely thought of fishing to calm himself down a little but he couldn't visualise the place, couldn't get past organising his tackle at the house. But then it was far too hot to look at the trees any more.

So he dove down deep into the water and found an underwater log to hold him down there. He must have burnt his other cheek because it was still hot under the water. He felt it for a long time and waited for the heat to pass over. But it didn't. *It would be so much easier if I didn't have to breathe*, he thought. *I could stay down here and wait. I could have run through the smoke too. It would have let me run clean through it and I'd be home already. Then I wouldn't be here worrying about breathing.*

He took a quick gulp of air and plunged back under. He was worried he'd lose his boot and bob up like a float, but it was a good hold he had under the log and there wasn't much current. He just had to keep his boot on and wedged under that log, otherwise he'd bob up into the flames.

For the first time he opened his eyes and saw it was dark and realised one side of his face was cool. *My hands are cool too*, he thought. *And my feet. And my back and my arms and my neck. Breathe,* he told himself. So he did and got burnt and coughed smoke and had to breathe again. Then he ducked back underwater—so cool and dark and with the good boot stuck under the log, but coughing the smoke had scared him. *If it fills the riverbed I am a goner.* He had a terrible moment of panic. *I don't want to die here,* he thought. *I want to die at the sea and have a little place and visit Murray whenever I want to. But if I die Flynn will teach him how to take the beatings and be a man.*

You won't die, he told himself. *All you do is wait and then run and keep the good boot under the log and breathe.*

It had been a while since he had breathed. He took another smoky breath and the panic came back and so did the thought of death. *Maybe it will be like getting drunk on rum. Then I won't really know it till I try and stand up. Still you have a good time on rum so if that is how you die I can't be dying.* He lay under the dark water and tried to relax so he wouldn't need to breathe as much. *Maybe death comes as darkness and you have to face it and watch for it and fight it off. That's probably why the old men go to bed late and get up so early.*

He opened his eyes and saw red.

I should see black in this water. The wall is on me now, he thought.

He took another breath and then stuck the good boot back under the log. He imagined the men saving the house. They'd have the other truck parked right in front of it with the water pumping out and all the trees near it cut down to keep it away from the fire. He felt so useless. He was the one who ought to be there with Michelle. *They'd feel obliged to help her with everything if I died,* he thought grimly. *You won't die,* he reassured himself. *The fire will burn over soon enough and then you can put the country under wheat. Then you can harvest it and pay Rawlings and give the place to Murray.* If only it had rained. Then he wouldn't have had to burn the trees. Now the country was sticking it to him for it. This must be his punishment for cutting Grandpa's trees. Grandpa and Dad always left the trees here.

You have violated Arbour, he told himself.

But God knows I'm sorry and will show me his heaven.

He cried a single tear into the river.

He realised he wasn't thinking straight and hadn't taken a breath. He hadn't dared go to the surface.

He bobbed out of the water again and stole another scalding breath. The wall was still above him. The trees had become fiery skeletons. Limbs fell to the earth. It was like the sun had fallen on him. The dirty water was red to look through, such was the intensity of the fire overhead.

He told himself to pull it together.

I can plant more trees, he thought angrily. *The bloody stuff grows back by itself anyway. I'll plant them myself if that is what this is all about.* Then he saw a little white house on the hill and a shed full of fishing poles. He saw the valley and fruit trees but got distracted because the current kept bumping slippery things into his legs and he didn't know what they were.

Probably perch or catfish, he thought, *or sticks, or reeds.*

It made him want to get out of the water more than ever but when he surfaced to breathe again the fire was the hottest he had felt it and he was sure he burnt off some of his hair even though it was wet. *I can't breathe that heat in*, he strained. There wouldn't be any air to breathe anyway. This must be the worst of it. He caught a reed with his left hand. *I ought to breath with the reed*, he thought. But he didn't use it straightaway because he knew it would just burn up.

Why doesn't it rain right now? he prayed.

Then I could go home. Then I could grow wheat. Then Murray could come home from the Territory and I could go to the sea. But when he tried to think of the sea he couldn't.

In fact he couldn't think of anything—just didn't think any more and stayed there in the water with the good boot stuck under the log and waited. He stayed like that for a long time.

Much later Flynn drove his two-wheeler through the burnt-out trees near the truck carcass. All of a sudden he heard a noise and was nearly bowled over by the rogue bullock. It came bolting out from nowhere and galloped past him like a mad thing. He watched its rump getting smaller and saw it disappearing and reappearing away through the tree skeletons. He didn't drive after it but towards an area where the fire had already burnt through.

Where the hell was Millvan? Flynn knew that the fire

had pissed Millvan off and that Millvan wouldn't back away from it. Then he'd get the shit smashed out of him like with the loggers and no one could tell him he was a fool. Flynn yelled out for him. Then he turned off the bike hoping he might hear a reply, but all he heard was the very distant crackling of the fire. He called out again and that was when the dog showed up.

'Come here,' said Flynn. The dog jumped onto the back of the bike, slobbering everywhere and covered in soot. 'What the fuck are you doing here?'

Flynn started up the bike again and continued on. Soon they came to a place close to the river and the dog howled and jumped off. Flynn couldn't see over the bank and fearfully stalled the bike. The dog was howling with a strange high pitch. Flynn let the bike fall as he got off it. He didn't even bother to prop it on the stand. The dog was barking now as if it was cornered by a snake.

Overhead the fire was dimming. The big trees by the river had turned to pointy smoking butts and the ground cover was just ash now. It was very smoky but the real heat had passed. Millvan could tell this because the red wasn't so bright through the muddy water. *It should be all right now,* he thought. He needed to breathe. He released his boot hold of the good log and took in a fiery breath that scalded him. It was still too hot.

So he panicked again and it was a long stress that turned his mind red as though it was on fire. It was red and hurt with a big fear in his chest. It was worse than in a bad dream because the pain was real, but then something burst and he fell into a calm. It was as though his mind had accepted the death that could take him. It was the calmest he had been all day and he was only glad for the luck he still had and didn't care if his house burnt down or even if he died. He didn't care about markets, banks or interest rates. Nothing was complicated—and *the calm*. There was his family and his mates to worry about but nothing else. It was the greatest calm he had ever known. He felt comfortably detached from the work and the fire. He didn't care about it anymore.

Millvan looked up from under the water again.

Soon I'll be able to get out of this river, he thought happily. *Soon I'll be able to run again*. He could almost feel himself moving already. Millvan lay there without thinking anything and waited. He watched the dark in his mind float by as red then yellow then green then clear. Then he watched the colours dissolve and become dark again. He had no idea how long he waited there in the dark but it was a good long time. He couldn't remember how long he'd been there before he got the calm.

A short time later there was a bird's foot in the water

beside him. It flew up when he went to touch it but he knew this time he could get a good big breath. *If the birds can breathe, it's alive up there again.*

First he brought his head out of the water and wiped his eyes to see the fire. It was gone. The air was fresh and the smoke had all but dissipated to a greenish haze. He smiled, the great calm still in him, and made for the closest bank.

He came out of the water slowly and saw himself moving with heavy motions. Even when he was out of the water he felt like he was still wading, like coming off a boat and still rocking on dry land. He felt his actions were slower and flowing. He walked on his toes with one bare foot but felt barely any contact with the ground at all. It would have been strange to him without the great calm.

He heard a faraway shouting. The others were standing on the bank laughing at him. He was covered in soot and the water was black. The men were black too and had streaks on their faces where they'd wiped at sweat. Donny told him he looked like a drowned rat and Flynn said they hadn't even had to chop the peppercorns away from close to the house. Then he told them what he'd done, how he'd breathed under the water with a reed, and they laughed and clapped him on the back. He told them how he had the idea to move underwater down stream and out of the fire's way. It was a good thought to have breathed with a reed till he felt it was cool enough for him to get out. He remembered it became cool very suddenly. He remembered the fire sweep away and the red turn purple, pink then blue. Cleared to blue in an instant. They clapped him on the back again and again. It reminded him of all those nights on the verandah, by a fire or at a clearing sale.

They explained to him Murray was already chopping at the stumps with a tomahawk.

'He's got through ten acres already,' they said together. 'You should see the crazy bastard go, he's so happy to be back here working again. He'll have it under wheat,' they said. 'He'll get it done,' they said. Their voices echoed. 'He doesn't need your help.'

He felt a wonderful sense of pride and laughed with them.

'I'll leave him to it then.'

He saw Michelle walking through the trees. She had a red dress on with a hibiscus pattern and was smiling and looked very beautiful. There was a way the red and yellow of her hair reminded him of something but he couldn't make his mind chase the idea. It was better just to watch her. He'd always loved that hair. She glowed with it and her smile was trim. *She's seen me and I must be wet-bedraggled.* But he wasn't, he'd taken his shirt off.

Then Michelle was right beside him and she was crying because he was all right and they hugged and the others must have got embarrassed because they said they'd go and help Murray and were gone before he had a chance to stop them. He couldn't yell after them either. Something kept him fixed on his wife. It was the greatest feeling he'd ever known. It split his working heart and the will of his hands left him. It was just Michelle and him. They walked through the stumps and got into the ute and started driving. She drove and he watched out the window like a little kid. The fire had done a very good job and the smoke had all blown away. The bush was burnt to flat and for the first time he saw a horizon that had been hidden all his life. Then they were nearing the house and every gate was open so they didn't need to stop. He could see the house very clearly, the big shady trees unscathed. He watched it from the road as they drove straight past. And Terry was waving to him out the window. He looked at him and shouted to him but Terry didn't hear him. He just waved and turned back inside. When they turned up the driveway with the sun behind them he knew where they were going. Up ahead it looked like rain and he hoped Donny would get a decent hit, but he didn't worry too much about it for right now he was going to the sea. He saw Michelle was smiling as she drove so he was sure he was right. He looked out the window and the country slipped by as sliding clear gaps in the bush. The air sucking in through the window seemed colder and fresher and the range loomed up in the distance. Rising up off the horizon it came slowly towards them as they drove.

They'd floated over the crest of the range now and it smelt of wet grasses and salt. The air was warmer through the window. He could see the little house on the hill, the valley and the fruit trees, and alongside trotted the dingo and further behind was that rangy rogue bullock.

Flynn ran through the smoke after the howling dog. It was frantic and whining a strange sound that Flynn had never heard a dog make before. Then he saw Millvan in the water. There were bubbles popping around his head and he was floating face down. The river was soot black and he was caught with his legs bunting two charred black logs. Flynn saw the bubbles and charged into the water.

'If there are bubbles I can pump air into him,' he muttered. 'Silly bastard!' He was crying. Flynn dragged him in his arms.

He got him out and onto the bank. He was all rolled back and dirty water seeped out of his nose like when you stamp on rock shellfish.

'You better stop crying,' Flynn told himself.

'Wake up you heavy bastard. You silly bastard.' He pumped at Millvan's chest but he didn't know if that was good or bad.

'Damn it.' The water was still running out Millvan's nose and he had to rub away his own tears to make sure.

Then the others turned up. Later on they explained they'd heard the dog's high-pitched howling.

Donny pelted down the riverbank and slid the last few metres. He took Millvan's head in his hands and tilted it to let the water run out better. It ran out black and sooty. He'd seen worse in Vietnam but it was on the very edge of his memory. It had been so very long since he had practised resuscitation.

'Take off his shirt!' Donny ordered.

Flynn was still crying.

'Take it off so I can see what I'm doing. Now! Do it quick.'

Flynn unbuttoned the shirt slowly.

'He's gone,' he moaned.

'Shut up!' yelled Donny. 'Get out of my way.'

Flynn wiped at his eyes and touched Millvan's head on Donny's lap.

'You bloody fool,' he whimpered, 'you're a goner.'

Donny breathed air into Millvan's lungs. 'One, two three, four, five . . . Out the bloody road!'

Flynn slumped away.

Donny pumped at his chest three times.

'Help me do this!' he yelled at Flynn. 'Breathe into his mouth. Do it every twenty seconds or so. Do it deep and then turn his head like I did.'

Flynn nodded.

When Flynn finished, Donny waited a little then pumped at Millvan's chest.

Flynn sobbed as Donny pumped.

Flynn was still sobbing and had his head in his big hands

when Millvan finally opened his eyes. Donny saw the glimmer of dull recognition and slid onto his backside in relief and horror at how close it had been. Flynn saw Donny prop backwards and gave a louder sob. Millvan turned his head towards Flynn. Donny nudged Flynn to look with his boot.

The first thing Millvan saw was Flynn's smiling red face. He blinked and felt the breeze on his own face and remembered being underwater. Now he felt himself gasping and choking on all the air. He felt a steadying arm holding him upright. Later he saw it was Donny's. He looked to his left and then slowly to the right, searching for Michelle, but she wasn't there.

'The fire is gone,' he said.

Flynn and Donny spoke over the top of each other in excitement to explain how they'd stopped the fire in the grass paddock and contained it before the house. The whole river block had ended up burning as they wanted. He didn't really hear them. His thoughts were entirely bent upon the burnt country. The will of his hands was slowly creeping back.

'I beat you, wind,' he said. In this battle anyway.

He took in the dirty water, smoking landscape and smiling mates. There was a lot to be done. Now he could grow wheat if they could prepare the soil in time. The ground was full of primed seeds and trees that would shoot with the first rain. He knew the country still had plenty of fight but he would meet it. That was the way of things.